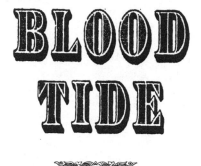

A NEVER LAND BOOK

Also by Dave Barry and Ridley Pearson

Peter and the Starcatchers
Peter and the Shadow Thieves
Peter and the Secret of Rundoon
Escape from the Carnivale
Cave of the Dark Wind

Also by Ridley Pearson

The Kingdom Keepers—Disney After Dark
Kingdom Keepers—Disney At Dawn
Steel Trapp: The Challenge

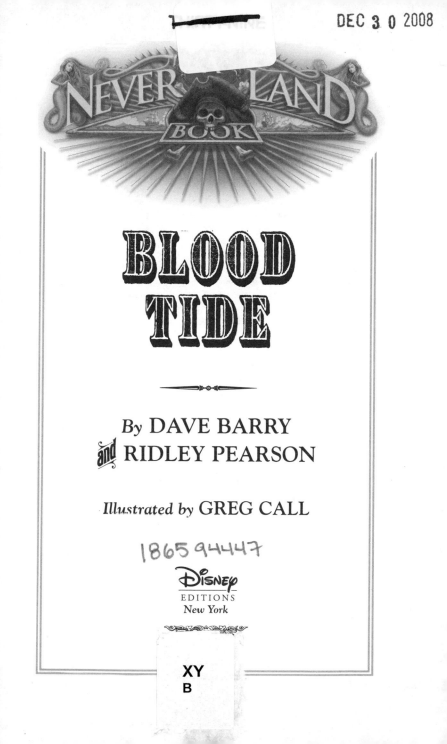

NEVER LAND BOOK

BLOOD TIDE

By DAVE BARRY
and RIDLEY PEARSON

Illustrated by GREG CALL

DISNEP
EDITIONS
New York

Copyright © 2008 Dave Barry and Page One, Inc.

For information address Disney Editions, 114 Fifth Avenue,
New York, New York 10011-5690.

Printed in the United States of America
Reinforced binding

First Edition
10 9 8 7 6 5 4 3 2 1

Library of Congress Cataloging-in-Publication Data on file.
ISBN 0-7868-3791-5

Dear Reader—

A little while back we wrote a book called *Peter and the Starcatchers*. It told the story of what happened to Peter Pan *before* he was Peter Pan and how he became a boy who could fly.

That book ended with Peter and his friends on an island with mermaids, pirates, and some natives who call themselves the Mollusk Tribe.

Right now, Peter is off having more adventures, and we're writing another book about those. But while he's gone, exciting things are happening to his friends—and his enemies—on the island. We decided it would be fun to tell some of those stories in a book for younger readers (like our own children). And so we wrote the book you're holding now. We hope you enjoy reading it as much as we enjoyed writing it.

Sincerely,

Dave Barry and Ridley Pearson

TABLE OF CONTENTS

CHAPTER 1: *Rolling Thunder*

CHAPTER 2: *Something Bit Me*

CHAPTER 3: *Kettle Point*

CHAPTER 4: *A Gift from the Sea Gods*

CHAPTER 5: *Flaming Hand Wades In*

CHAPTER 6: *The Warrior Council*

CHAPTER 7: *The Mermaids Strike*

CHAPTER 8: *Borrowing a Canoe*

CHAPTER 9: *Bubbles Rising*

CHAPTER 10: *A Strategic Genius*

CHAPTER 11: *Movement on the Mountainside*

CHAPTER 12: *Teacher Speaks*

CHAPTER 13: *Escape*

CHAPTER 14: *Devil's Hole*

CHAPTER 15: *The Chief's Clever Plan*

CHAPTER 16: *The Children Grow Weary*

CHAPTER 17: *There Won't Be Nothing Left*

CHAPTER 18: *The Water Turns White*

CHAPTER 19: *Rolling Boulders*

CHAPTER 20: *It Might Hold A Pig*

CHAPTER 21: *The Battle Raged*

CHAPTER 22: *Bowling For Pirates*

CHAPTER 23: *Nowhere to Run*

CHAPTER 24: *Falling Water*

CHAPTER 25: *The Rising Wave*

CHAPTER 26: *Blub Blub Blub*

CHAPTER 27: *The Best Day*

CHAPTER 1

ROLLING THUNDER

THE DETERMINED RAYS OF SUNRISE crept across
the Mollusk Island jungle and found their way
into a hollow tree stump, which led down into an
underground hideaway. As the soft dawn light
penetrated the darkness, it revealed four small boys
asleep in hammocks. Two of them—Tubby Ted and
Thomas—were on their backs, snoring; another,
Prentiss, was curled up against the slight chill in the
morning air.

The fourth boy, James, was on his stomach, his
legs and arms sticking out to the sides, his posture
matching his dream. He was flying, just like Peter,

who was off in England, visiting his Starcatcher friend Molly Aster, having adventures, saving the world.

In his dream, it was James having the adventures, not Peter; he soared like an eagle as swords clanged and cannons rumbled and boomed below. It all seemed so real . . . especially the rumbling of the cannons.

Suddenly James's eyes flicked open. He wasn't dreaming: the rumbling was *real*. The boy's underground hideaway was shaking. Clods of dirt and chunks of lava were falling from the ceiling and walls. His hammock was swinging the way hammocks swing on ships.

"Wake up!" shouted James, clambering out of his hammock. "Wake up!"

Prentiss uncurled; Tubby Ted snorted himself awake; Thomas grunted, wiped some drool from his chin, and sat up, immediately falling out of his hammock. Ordinarily this would have made the others laugh. But the whole hideaway was shaking now, and the deep rumbling sound was everywhere, all around them, terrifyingly loud.

"What's happening?" shouted Tubby Ted.

"I've no idea," replied James. "But we have to get out of here."

He started toward the stick ladder that led up to the stump-hole, but staggered and fell, the movement of the floor making it almost impossible to walk. As Tubby Ted tried to climb from his hammock, one of the pegs holding it up pulled loose from the vibrating wall. The hammock dropped, and Ted plummeted to the dirt floor.

As the four boys struggled to stand, water began seeping, and then gushing through one of the walls. The hideaway was flooding!

On hands and knees, all four boys scrambled for the ladder. Thomas reached it and managed to get up to the stump; he shoved it aside. Blinding sunlight streamed inside. Whatever was causing the horrible noise, it wasn't thunder.

Thomas climbed out, followed by Tubby Ted and Prentiss. James was last up the ladder, and as he climbed, the earth shook so ferociously that the ladder snapped in two. Thomas caught James's hands and, with the help of the other boys, managed to pull him out of the hole.

Beneath their feet the ground was heaving and

buckling; overhead, the massive trees were swaying violently; the deep rumble seemed to be coming from everywhere.

"It's an . . . earthshake," Thomas said

"Earth*quake*," Prentiss corrected.

A dozen yards away, a massive tree toppled with a loud crash. Then another came down, this one even closer to the boys. The jungle seemed to be coming apart before their eyes. A palm tree crashed to the ground, flinging its coconuts sideways; one struck Tubby Ted and knocked him to the ground. As the boys helped up Tubby Ted, James shouted, "To the beach! We've got to get away from the trees!"

Staggering and stumbling on the heaving ground, dodging falling trees and branches, the boys ran down a jungle path toward the water. They could see that the sea—usually calm—was wild this morning, with huge waves surging toward shore.

Suddenly, just as the boys reached the beach, the rumbling and shaking stopped. They turned and looked back at the jungle: it was a tangled mass of fallen and leaning trees. For a few seconds there was no sound except that of the waves sliding up the sand.

And then, in the distance, they heard a haunting sound, like a mournful trumpet. It was the sound of a conch shell, the signal used by the Mollusk Tribe, the native people who had given the island its name. The Mollusks were friends of the boys, protecting them from Captain Hook and his pirates, who lived on the other side of the island. The boys recognized the signal: it was the call to meet at the Mollusk village.

The boys started trotting down the beach toward the sound. The trot turned into a run as another tremor began to shake the beach, almost turning the sand underfoot into liquid. The ocean waves became thundering mountains of water, crashing onto the shore as if determined to wash the island away forever.

CHAPTER 2

SOMETHING BIT ME

THE GROUND STOPPED SHAKING just as the boys
reached the Mollusk village. Within a few minutes,
the sea was also calm. But the Mollusk chief,
Fighting Prawn, insisted that the boys remain inside
the village walls, along with most of the tribe, while
he and some of the elders inspected the island. They
returned a few hours later to report that, other than
toppling many trees, the earthquake appeared to
have caused little serious damage.

It had, however, made a soggy mess of the boys'
underground hideaway. Fighting Prawn invited the
boys to sleep in a hut in the village while their home

was drying out. The boys accepted the offer readily; they liked being close to their friends Shining Pearl and Little Scallop, daughters of the chief. They also appreciated the Mollusk's cooking—fish, wild pig, and other treats. When the boys got their own food, they tended to eat whatever was lying around, which meant on many days they ate coconut for breakfast, lunch, and supper.

To repay their hosts for their hospitality, the boys spent most of the next day helping the Mollusks clear the fallen trees and branches that had blocked many of the paths through the jungle. When the work was done, the boys, along with Shining Pearl and Little Scallop, headed down to the lagoon to cool off with an afternoon swim.

Prentiss was the first to emerge from the jungle onto the beach. As soon as he saw the water he stopped so quickly that Thomas, who was right behind and in a hurry to go swimming, bumped into him.

"Hey, watch out!" said Thomas.

"Look at the water," said Prentiss, pointing.

Thomas looked, and his mouth opened in surprise. "It's the wrong color," he said. Now the other children, emerging from the jungle, saw it, too. The lagoon—usually a clear, brilliant sunlit blue—was a murky reddish color, like rust.

"What's happened to the lagoon?" said Tubby Ted, addressing the question to Shining Pearl, who had lived on the island the longest.

"I don't know," said Shining Pearl. "I've never seen it look like this before."

"Me, either," said Little Scallop.

"Maybe the earthquake did it," suggested James. "Stirred up the mud on the bottom."

"Maybe," said Shining Pearl, frowning. "Although there isn't much mud in the lagoon, is there?"

"No," admitted James. "There isn't." His eyes drifted out to the big rock in the lagoon. It was known as Mermaid Rock, because the mermaids often could be seen sunning themselves on it. James saw three of them out there, but they weren't lying on the rock; they were in the water next to it, with only their heads visible. The sun was behind them, so he couldn't make out their faces. He waved, but the mermaids—normally friendly and outgoing—did not wave back. James started to wonder about that, but his thoughts were interrupted by Thomas.

"Are we going swimming, then?" he said, starting toward the water.

"D'you think we should?" said Prentiss, aiming his question mostly at James, who was the leader of the boys when Peter was away.

"I dunno," said James. "Maybe we should ask Fighting Prawn."

"What for?" said Thomas, who had reached the lagoon and was starting to wade into the murky water. "Are you afraid?"

"No, I'm not afraid," said James, reddening and glancing at Shining Pearl.

"Then come on," said Thomas. He took two steps and dove into the water. He surfaced a few yards farther out, shook the water from his hair, and shouted, "It's fine!"

James hesitated. He didn't like the looks of the water. But he *was* hot, and he certainly didn't want anybody, especially Shining Pearl, to think he was not brave.

"All right, then," he said, walking toward the water. In a minute, all six children were splashing and laughing in the lagoon. Despite its unusual appearance, the water felt as refreshing as ever; the children quickly forgot their concerns. Gradually their frolicking took them from knee-high water, to waist-high, and then deeper.

"Let's race to Mermaid Rock!" shouted Thomas.

James looked out toward the rock. It was empty; the three mermaids he'd seen earlier were gone. He was about to say something, but the race was already on: Thomas, a fine swimmer, was stroking swiftly through the water toward the rock, with the other children following as fast as they could. James, determined not to be the last to reach the rock, dove toward the rock and began swimming.

He had taken three strokes when he heard the scream. He thrust himself as high out of the water as he could and scanned the area ahead. Another scream. It was coming from Thomas.

"My leg!" he shouted. "Something bit me!"

James began swimming toward Thomas as fast as he could.

"Help!" shouted Thomas. "It's . . ."

As James watched in horror, Thomas's head disappeared below the surface.

"What's happening?" shouted Prentiss from somewhere off to James's right. "Where's Thomas?"

"Get back to the beach!" shouted James. "Tell the others!"

Flailing his arms furiously, James reached the spot where Thomas had disappeared. He took a breath and dove down. In the murky water, he could not see far, but he caught sight of something beneath him—it was Thomas's pale face, looking up toward him, eyes wide in fright: he was reaching up. With two thrusts of his arms, James dove down close enough to grab Thomas's hands. James changed direction and thrust upward, trying to pull Thomas to the surface. But something was holding his friend down. James's lungs burned; he couldn't stay down much longer.

James saw a shape flash past him, diving deep . . . Shining Pearl! She was a superb swimmer, better than any of the boys. She dove down toward Thomas's legs. There was a swirl of motion, and suddenly Thomas was free. As James lunged toward the surface, pulling Thomas with him, he saw some shapes flash past; he caught a glimpse of flowing blond hair and a long, graceful green tail.

His head broke the surface, and he gulped air as he yanked up Thomas next to him, gasping and coughing. A second later, Shining Pearl's head appeared.

"Get him to shore!" she shouted. "It's the mermaids!"

Before James could say anything, Pearl was diving down again. James felt something cold grab his leg; he shouted and kicked as hard as he could. Whatever it was let go. Holding Thomas with one arm and stroking furiously with the other, James swam toward shore. When his feet could feel sand he stood and put Thomas's arm over his shoulder.

The two of them stumbled out of the shallow water and onto the beach. Thomas lay on the sand, coughing and spitting up water. Prentiss, Tubby Ted, and Little Scallop ran to them.

"What happened?" said Prentiss.

"I don't know," said James. "Shining Pearl said . . . Wait! Where is Shining Pearl?"

"Here she comes!" said Little Scallop.

They looked out and saw Shining Pearl swimming hard toward them, pausing every few strokes to flail her arms at something behind her. She reached the shallow water and began to run. Behind her a mermaid's head rose from the water, then another, then a third; their normally lovely faces were twisted in anger. For a moment they hissed and snarled, revealing their sharp mermaid teeth. Then, with a flash of green tails, they turned and disappeared beneath the lagoon's murky surface.

Shining Pearl stumbled ashore.

"Are you all right?" asked James.

"Yes," she gasped. "What about Thomas?"

"I'm all right, I think," Thomas said. "One of them bit my leg." He pointed to his right leg, where there was a ring of bright red tooth marks.

"What on earth got into them?" said James. "They've never done anything like this!"

"No," said Shining Pearl gazing out at the lagoon. "They haven't."

"So what should we do?" said Tubby Ted.

"We should tell father," said Little Scallop.

"Yes," agreed Shining Pearl. "And right away."

The six children trotted up the beach and into the jungle. James was last in line. As he reached the jungle's edge, he looked back at the lagoon. Once again, there were three heads in the water next to Mermaid Rock. James could not make out the mermaids' faces. But there was no doubt in his mind that they were watching him.

CHAPTER 3

KETTLE POINT

AT FIRST, FIGHTING PRAWN did not believe the children.

"The mermaids have always been friendly," he said. "Are you sure it wasn't a fish that attacked you?" He smiled in a way that made Shining Pearl very angry; she *hated* it when her father didn't take her seriously.

"Father, I know what a fish looks like!" she said. "Do you know any fish that leaves bite marks like those?" She pointed at Thomas's leg. Fighting Prawn bent down and inspected the rows of red marks. He nodded, frowning.

"You're right," he said. "That's not a fish bite."

Shining Pearl made a *hmph* sound.

"The teeth didn't break the skin," said Fighting Prawn. "Are you all right, Thomas?"

"I'm fine, sir," said Thomas, adding, in his bravest voice, "it was nothing."

"No," said Fighting Prawn. "It was something, and I mean to find out what." He rose and ordered a scouting party of four warriors to go to Mermaid Lagoon and see what the mermaids were up to. Under no circumstances, he told them, were they to go into the water.

"That goes for you children, as well," he said. "You're to stay away from the lagoon."

"But it's hot," said Prentiss. "Can't we swim somewhere else?" The other children, including Thomas, nodded. It *was* hot.

"What about Kettle Point?" said Little Scallop. This was a point near Skull Rock where hot springs bubbled from the ground. There was a fine beach there.

"Oh, father," said Shining Pearl, "can we go to Kettle Point? There's no mermaids there."

Fighting Prawn considered this. "Well, I suppose so," he said. "If you're careful."

The children nodded vigorously.

"While you're there," said Fighting Prawn, "see what damage the earthquake did on that side of the island."

"Like a scouting party!" said Prentiss.

"Yes," said Fighting Prawn. "You'll be a scouting party."

Happy with their new mission, the children set off toward Kettle Point. As they neared the beach, Tubby Ted spotted a mango tree and left the trail in search of a snack. As he approached the tree, he suddenly stopped.

"Psst!" he called back to the others.

"No thanks, not hungry," said James.

"Shhh!" hissed Ted. He motioned for the others to come quietly. They formed a single file and crept through the jungle toward Ted. As they reached the mango tree, they heard what he'd heard: voices. Beyond the tree, the jungle gave way to beach grass where lizards scampered. Beyond that lay the sparkling, gray volcanic sand that covered the shore near Skull Rock.

Small waves lapped at the beach near a small spit of land where a circle of rocks surrounded a series of steaming pools: Kettle Point. But it was to the line of crashing surf out at the reef, well past Kettle Point, where Ted now pointed. The children looked there and saw where the voices were coming from.

"Pirates!" said Shining Pearl.

Six of Captain Hook's ragged men—who normally did not venture to this part of the island—were wading in the surf, snatching up objects being carried ashore by the waves. Two of them were struggling with a large hatch cover.

"A shipwreck! " said James.

Ted nodded enthusiastically. The pirates were carrying the shipwreck debris onto the beach, where they had made a stack of wood, pulleys, rope, and other objects.

"What are they going to do with it?" said Prentiss.

"They'll use it in their fort," said James. "Or let it dry and burn it. Pirates are clever."

"Look!" said Shining Pearl. "Over there!"

Three of the pirates had gathered around a small wooden keg. They appeared to be quite excited about it, waving the others over to see. The others came over, and they, too, celebrated the find.

"What do you suppose it is?" said Tubby Ted.

"We need to get closer," said Thomas.

Shining Pearl shook her head. "We're not supposed to go near the pirates," she said.

"She's right," said James.

"What," said Thomas. "Are you afraid?"

"Of course I'm not," snapped James, his face reddening.

"Well then, let's have a look," said Thomas.

James hesitated.

"I think I know what it is," said Ted. He pointed toward the pirates. One of them had hoisted the keg onto his shoulder, and was lugging it up the beach, with the others following.

"What?" said James.

"They had kegs like that on the ship," said Ted. "Remember?"

James frowned.

"Next to the cannons," said Ted.

"Powder," James said.

"Black powder," Ted said proudly. "That's why they're so excited."

"That's dangerous," Shining Pearl said.

"We don't know it's black powder," said Thomas. "We need to get closer."

The pirate carrying the keg was heading up the beach toward the jungle, with the others right behind.

"Let's follow," said Thomas.

"We need to tell father," said Shining Pearl.

"No time," said Thomas.

"But we came over here to swim," reminded Little Scallop.

"I'm going," said Thomas. "Who's with me?"

James bit his lower lip, then reluctantly said, "I'm in."

Shining Pearl scolded him with her eyes.

"If it *is* black powder," James told her, "it's important we know what they're up to. These are pirates, after all!"

She sighed and said, "All right. You'd get lost without me anyway."

The others all nodded; they'd go as a group. With Thomas leading the way, they plunged into the jungle. Shining Pearl was second in line. She glanced over her shoulder at James with a look that said what they were both thinking: *we should NOT be doing this.*

CHAPTER 4

A GIFT FROM THE SEA GODS

THE CHILDREN TROTTED ALONG the jungle path as quietly as they could, trying to stay just out of sight of the pirates. The pirates made the job easier by not looking behind them; they were too excited about the wooden keg they'd found in the shipwreck debris.

After a half hour the pirates stopped for a rest. James crouched and hand-signaled the other children to slip into the jungle, so as not to be seen. Ted stepped right into a sticky web and fought the gooey silk off his face, as an enormous spider dangled in front of his eyes. If James had not clapped a hand over Ted's mouth, half the island might have heard him cry out.

James and Thomas seized the opportunity to sneak closer to the pirates, hoping to determine the contents of the keg. But just as they drew near, the pirates rose from their resting places and took off again. The children scrambled to catch up and were soon following at a safe distance once more but with no better idea of what it was they were following.

They came to Clear Creek, which was running higher than usual. The pirates crossed it carefully, taking pains to keep the keg as dry as possible. When the pirates had disappeared into the jungle on the other side, the children approached the creek. Thomas stepped right into the rushing water and was almost carried away by the strong current. But he caught his balance and, half swimming, managed to make it across. James and the others stopped at the edge.

"Past here is pirate territory," James called across.

"I thought you wanted to know what was in the keg," answered Thomas. "Are you afraid?"

James's ears burned. "Course not," he said.

"Then come on!" said Thomas.

"We should tell Father," Shining Pearl said.

"Yes," agreed James, looking across at Thomas. "But it *is* important to know what's in that keg."

"I'm staying here," said Prentiss.

"Me, too," said Ted, eyeing the churning water.

James and Shining Pearl looked at each other, then at Thomas across the creek. Shining Pearl sighed and turned to Prentiss, Ted, and Little Scallop.

"Don't you *dare* say anything to Father until we're back," she said. "Promise?"

"Promise," they answered together.

Shining Pearl eased into the roiling water and made her way across, struggling to keep her balance. She'd never seen the water this high. Thomas offered her a hand on the other side, pulling her up to dry ground. James followed across a moment later.

"We won't be long," James called across to Ted, Prentiss, and Little Scallop. "Wait for us at the hut, and whatever you do, don't go near the lagoon."

Turning away from the creek, James, Thomas, and Shining Pearl set off into the jungle. After a mile of fast walking they came to the edge of the clearing where the pirates had built their fort. It looked as though a strong wind might blow it down, but in fact it had weathered some ferocious storms. The uneven wall, made of driftwood and palm-tree trunks lashed together with vine, met at a large, reinforced gate. At the moment the gate was open, though it could be closed quickly in case of an attack by Mr. Grin, the giant crocodile who always lurked nearby.

Peering through the jungle leaves, the children could see past the open gate into the compound. They saw fish drying on a rack and a small fire wearing a gray hat of spiraling smoke, but no people.

Needing a better view, they crept through the jungle to a spot nearer the wall, where they climbed a massive, vine-covered tree high enough so that they could see into the compound. There they saw the pirates with the keg gathered outside a ramshackle shack. As they watched, a tall, thin man with a hard face and a vast moustache emerged from the shack. He stepped into the sunlight, shielding his eyes with the stump of an arm at the end of which was a sword fashioned into a hook. This was Captain Hook, who had once been the most feared

pirate on the seas. He looked at the keg with piercing black eyes.

"What's this?" he snarled.

"A bit of treasure, Cap'n," said one of the men, named Hurky. "From a shipwreck."

The other five pirates nodded in agreement.

"What kind of treasure?" said Hook.

Hurky spun the keg around so Hook could see something written on its side. His eyes lit up, and he very nearly managed to smile. Clearly he was pleased. But from the tree, the children couldn't see what it was that Hook had read on the side of the keg.

"Washed ashore at Kettle Point," said Hurky. "We snatched it up before them Mollusks could get it."

"A gift from the sea gods," said Hook. "Have you tested it?"

Hurky shook his head. "We brung it here straightaways," he said.

"Pull the bung!" ordered Hook.

Hurky and another man used a rock and a long nail to dislodge a corklike piece of wood in the top of the keg. Hurky lifted the keg and carefully poured something into Hook's outstretched hand. The group of pirates parted as Hook walked toward the smoldering fire. He held his hand out into the curl of smoke, looked up at his men, and then opened his fist.

The fire flashed a brilliant white. The pirates jumped back as a thick twist of black smoke rose into the air—all but Hook, who stood over the fire, his hatchet face widened by a smile revealing twin rows of brown, crooked teeth.

"Now this . . ." he said, glittering dark eyes on the rising smoke, ". . .this changes everything."

CHAPTER 5

FLAMING HAND
WADES IN

FLAMING HAND COULD STAND the heat no longer. He was one of four Mollusk warriors assigned to watch the lagoon under the blazing summer sun. By the middle of the day, you could cook a fish just by laying it on a rock.

Fighting Prawn had warned his men not to swim in the lagoon. But Flaming Hand was never one to follow orders precisely (he'd been given his name after playing with fish oil too close to the fire). He was thinking that he wouldn't have to *swim* to cool off—just wade in knee deep. How could some fish girl hurt a Mollusk warrior, anyway?

Determined to cool off, he stepped into the cloudy water. He could feel the eyes of the other three warriors, squatting in the shade of the palm trees, watching him closely. Suddenly, Flaming Hand made a terrified face and sank into the water, screaming. The other warriors leaped to their feet and ran toward the water, only to stop in disgust when Flaming Hand rose to his feet, laughing. They had fallen for his prank.

Flaming Hand waded a bit deeper; the water was murky, but refreshingly cool. He lowered himself until the water was up to his neck. He looked toward the shore, smiling to let the others know how good the water felt.

Suddenly the three men on the shore were shouting at him to get out. They pointed frantically at the water behind him. Flaming Hand nodded and smiled. He figured they were trying to trick him, as he had tricked them. But he wasn't going to fall for it. He didn't turn around. Instead, he waved at them, laughing.

Then he heard a splash behind him, and his laugh became a scream as he felt needle-sharp teeth sink into his leg.

CHAPTER 6

THE WARRIOR COUNCIL

SHINING PEARL AND LITTLE SCALLOP both noticed it at the same time—a gentle snoring sound from just outside the hut. Their mother had fallen asleep. They looked at each other, both thinking the same thing: this was their chance to sneak out and eavesdrop on the warrior council.

The girls were being punished. When they'd returned with the boys to the Mollusk camp, they expected to be praised for finding out about the pirates and their mysterious barrel. Instead, Fighting Prawn had been furious at them for following the pirates. He wasn't interested in the barrel; he said it was probably just grog, which pirates loved to drink. Shining Pearl and James tried to argue that what they saw was powder, not liquid, but Fighting Prawn wouldn't listen; his mind was on other problems. He ordered Shining Pearl and Little Scallop to spend the rest of the day in the hut, weaving mats. Then he went off to the warrior council, a meeting of the Mollusk warriors called by Fighting Prawn to discuss the mermaid attacks. Children were not allowed at the warrior council, but Shining Pearl and Little Scallop wanted badly to find out what was going on.

They tiptoed out of the hut, past their dozing mother. They sneaked around several other huts, ducked through the fish-drying racks, and came up behind the warrior lodge. There, they found a half-dozen other children—all boys—who had also ignored the rules, so they could listen in on the council. Peering through cracks in the lodge's stick walls, they saw two dozen men gathered in a semicircle, facing Fighting Prawn. He wore the chief's crown: a jagged piece of rare blue coral encrusted with "hard rock"—what the foreigners called diamonds—as well as some sea urchins and dried fish eyes. The largest eye, the size of a fist, was centered on Fighting

Prawn's forehead. As his daughters watched through the crack, Fighting Prawn tapped a stick on a conch shell, indicating the council was starting.

"As you know," he said, "the mermaids have attacked again. This time the victim was Flaming Hand. His legs were bitten badly in the lagoon. He will recover, but this is the second time the mermaids have attacked. I called this council so we can discuss how we will respond."

A warrior rose to his feet. This was Snapping Turtle, Flaming Hand's older brother, known for his temper.

"What is there to discuss?" he said. "Mollusks have been attacked. A Mollusk warrior's blood has been spilled."

"A Mollusk warrior who was in the lagoon against my orders," said Fighting Prawn.

"So what?" said Snapping Turtle, in a defiant tone rarely—if ever—used to address Fighting Prawn. "It's *our* island. It's *our* lagoon. We can't allow these *she*-fish to decide where we go. I say we spear them all."

Murmurs of agreement rippled through the warriors. Heads nodded.

Fighting Prawn stared at the warriors until they

fell silent. "I agree that we must respond," he said. "But not that we must kill the mermaids. We have lived next to them for some time now. They have helped us; they have been our friends and allies. Something has gone wrong, yes. But nobody has died. So let us first try to solve the problem in a peaceful manner."

"Peaceful?" said Snapping Turtle. "They attack my brother, and you want to do *nothing?*"

"No," said Fighting Prawn. "I want to find out what is causing this. I want to talk to the leader of the mermaids, the one called Teacher."

"Talk," said Snapping Turtle. He spat on the dirt floor, drawing a gasp from the other warriors, who had never seen such a lack of respect for the chief.

For a long few seconds, Fighting Prawn was silent. When he spoke, it was with a voice that did not allow for disagreement.

"Yes," he said. "Talk. And then, if necessary, action. But first, I will speak with Teacher. And you will do nothing until I say otherwise. Do you understand?"

Snapping Turtle glared at the chief and said nothing. The hut was silent, the warriors still as statues.

"Do you understand?"

Snapping Turtle nodded slowly, once. "I understand," he said softly. "I understand that Mollusk blood has been shed." He held out his hand, showing the others that he held a piece of lava in his palm. He clenched his fist, crumbling the lava. Dust slipped through his fingers and fell to the floor. He blew the remaining dust from his hand, then turned to the seated warriors and said, "I don't know about the rest of you, but I believe that when we are attacked, we fight back. I *will* avenge my brother."

"You will do," said Fighting Prawn slowly, "what your chief tells you to do."

By way of answer, Snapping Turtle turned and walked out of the lodge. Four other warriors stood and followed him out.

Fighting Prawn watched them go. Then he spoke with a mixture of sadness and anger.

"Snapping Turtle is upset because of his brother," he said. "I understand that. But he and the others who left must be disciplined for the disrespect they have shown this council." The warriors nodded, and Fighting Prawn continued: "For now, however, I must deal with the threat to our tribe posed by the

mermaids. I will go to see Teacher, with my sons."
Again, the warriors nodded. Fighting Prawn tapped
the conch shell again, indicating that the warrior
council was over.

After the council broke up, Fighting Prawn
headed down the path to the Mermaid Lagoon, followed by his sons, Bold Abalone and Sturdy Conch.
The children who had been eavesdropping on the
council scurried away from the warrior lodge, so as
not to be caught. Shining Pearl and Little Scallop
ducked behind a hut. They heard voices, and, peek-
ing around a corner, saw Snapping Turtle walking
past, with the other four warriors who had walked
out.

"I don't care if he's the chief," Snapping Turtle
was saying. "He's an old man, and he has lost his
fighting spirit."

The others nodded.

"He wants to talk," continued Snapping Turtle.
"But I say the time for talk is past. The she-fish have
attacked us twice. I say we fight back *now*."

The others muttered in agreement. With
Snapping Turtle leading the way, they plunged into
the jungle in the direction of the mermaid lagoon.

"This is terrible," Shining Pearl whispered to Little Scallop. "They're going to kill the mermaids! We must warn Father!"

"We should warn Teacher, too," said Little Scallop, "if we can find her before Snapping Turtle does."

"We'll get James and the others to help us," said Shining Pearl.

The two girls set off running as fast as they could, hoping desperately that it would be fast enough.

CHAPTER 7

THE MERMAIDS STRIKE

FIGHTING PRAWN AND HIS TWO SONS, Bold Abalone and Sturdy Conch, strode onto the hot, sunlit beach of Mermaid Lagoon. The sons carried a canoe, which they set down at the water's edge. They were about to climb in when Fighting Prawn stopped them.

"I must go alone," he said. "If the mermaids see two warriors and a chief, they might think we mean to fight."

"They might think that anyway," said Bold Abalone, gesturing back up the beach. Fighting Prawn looked and saw that the warriors who'd been in the council had gathered at the edge of the jungle, armed with spears. As he watched, a smaller group emerged from the jungle farther up the beach: Snapping Turtle and the other four warriors. They, too, held spears, and they were clearly planning to use them.

Fighting Prawn realized that he was close to losing control of all his warriors. He climbed into the canoe.

"It's too dangerous!" said Sturdy Conch. "Let us go with you!"

"No," said Fighting Prawn, in a tone of voice that his sons had never disobeyed and never would. "Now give me a push, before Snapping Turtle and the others make this situation worse than it already is."

His sons gave the canoe a shove, and Fighting Prawn shot out into the murky lagoon. He had never seen the water so cloudy. He slipped the paddle into the water and expertly propelled the canoe toward the center of the lagoon. Ahead he saw several mermaids on the rocks by Mermaid Island. Even at a distance, Fighting Prawn could tell something was wrong: the mermaids' faces, usually happy and welcoming, were grim; their eyes were narrowed to suspicious slits.

Fighting Prawn stopped paddling, raised his arm, and waved. The mermaids did not wave back. One of them slid swiftly off the rock into the water. She flipped her powerful tail and was gone. Fighting Prawn scanned the rocks, looking for Teacher, the mermaid leader. He had dealt with her before and felt that if he could just speak to her he could get to the bottom of the problem.

Once again, he started paddling toward the island. Suddenly, he spotted twin disturbances in the lagoon's calm surface, heading directly for him. He glanced over his shoulder at his sons on shore. They stood at the water's edge, their full attention focused on him. Fighting Prawn wondered if he'd made a mistake leaving them behind. . . .

The two mermaids struck. They hit the canoe with tremendous force, both on the right side, clearly intending to flip it. It was only through great quickness and balance that Fighting Prawn managed to shift his weight enough to keep the small craft from going over. He grabbed the sides, lowered himself into the bottom, and braced for the next attack.

It came quickly, the two mermaids hitting on the left side of the canoe. Again, the canoe rolled sharply, and this time Fighting Prawn couldn't prevent it from taking on water. Before Fighting Prawn could bail it out, the mermaids hit again and then again, each time rocking the canoe violently, so that more water poured in. Fighting Prawn heard shouting from his sons and the others onshore. But he was too busy fighting for his life to answer. He raised the paddle, watching as another disturbance in the

water streaked toward the canoe. He saw a flash of green tail, a stream of blond hair.

He brought the paddle down like an axe.

He heard a muted scream. Bubbles churned the water.

The other mermaid attacked from the same side, but Fighting Prawn was expecting it. Again he swung the paddle down; again he heard a cry of pain. For a moment he had driven off the attackers. He began paddling as hard as he could toward shore, grateful that the canoe, though carrying a foot of water, was still upright.

As he paddled he glanced back over his left shoulder, then his right. More water streaks were coming toward him; the mermaids had not given up. Again and again, he slashed at the water with his paddle, driving them away; again and again they came at him, sometimes getting close enough to rock the canoe. But now Fighting Prawn had help: his sons had gone back for and then launched a second canoe and were paddling furiously his way. They reached him in seconds and were lunging at the mermaids with the sharp tips of their spears. One of the mermaids raised her head and tried to bite the spear, revealing a frightening row of razor-sharp, pointed teeth. She snapped the spear in two.

But with the help of his sons, Fighting Prawn was soon able to reach the safety of shallow water. The mermaids, hissing in anger, had to turn away. Fighting Prawn and his sons dragged the canoes onto the beach. The other warriors, including Snapping Turtle's group, gathered around them. Fighting Prawn wiped the sweat from his brow and thanked his sons for coming to his rescue. Then he turned to face the others. Snapping Turtle stepped forward.

"Are you done with talking?" he said. "Are you ready to fight back?"

Fighting Prawn was silent for a moment. He looked at Mermaid Island; he could see a half dozen mermaids sitting on their rocks, watching. Then he turned back to the warriors.

"Yes," he said. "We will fight back."

A cheer went up, echoing across the lagoon to the watching mermaids.

CHAPTER 8

BORROWING A CANOE

SHINING PEARL AND LITTLE SCALLOP found the boys waiting just outside the village walls.

"What's happening?" said James. "What did they decide?"

"It's awful," said Shining Pearl. "They're going to attack the mermaids."

"And kill them," said Little Scallop, tears in her eyes.

"I'm not surprised," said Thomas. "After all, the mermaids have gone mad, attacking everyone who goes into the water."

James nodded. "But still," he said, "they've been

our friends. They've helped us more than once. *And* saved Peter's life."

The boys all nodded at that; the mermaids had indeed been very good friends in the past.

"Is there anything we can do?" said James.

"We've got to stop this," said Shining Pearl.

"How are you going to do that?" asked Ted.

"If we can talk to Teacher," said Shining Pearl, "and tell her what's happening, maybe she can get the other mermaids to come to their senses."

"But how do we get to Teacher?" said James.

"In a canoe," said Shining Pearl.

"But what about the mermaids?" said Ted, glancing nervously in the direction of the lagoon. "What if they attack the canoe?"

"We'll bring extra paddles," said James. "Some of us can fight off the mermaids while the others paddle."

"Um," said Ted. "Maybe one of us should stay on the beach, to stand guard and signal if there's trouble."

James looked at Ted and, with the slightest of smiles, said, "Good idea, Ted. Perhaps you could do that."

"If you insist," said Ted, looking relieved.

"Excuse me," said Prentiss. "But has anyone considered the fact that we don't have a canoe?"

"We're going to borrow one," said Shining Pearl.

"We?" said Prentiss.

"You boys are," said Shining Pearl, "while Little Scallop and I distract Father and the others."

She explained her plan to the boys. A few minutes later they had taken up their positions. Thomas was crouched outside the wall around the Mollusk village, peering through a crack at Fighting Prawn and his warriors. The other boys were hiding in the trees near where the Mollusks kept their canoes.

As Ted watched, Shining Pearl and Little Scallop approached their father. Fighting Prawn was explaining how they would attack the mermaid's island.

"Father!" said Shining Pearl.

He turned to face them, angry at the interruption.

"What is it?" he said.

"That barrel we told you about—the one the pirates found. I talked to James, and he's sure it wasn't grog. He says it must be gunpowder, because of the way it burned when—"

"Be quiet!" said Fighting Prawn, furious at his daughters' behavior. "Can you not see we are discussing a serious matter? I will deal with the pirates later. I will also deal with the two of you, who have disappointed me deeply." His dark eyes glared at his daughters. Shining Pearl felt terribly guilty for deceiving her father this way, but she also was glad to note that the eyes of all the warriors were on her, which meant that they would not be looking through the open village gate to where the canoes were kept. She hoped that Thomas had noticed this, as well.

He had. Outside the wall, Thomas was waving his arm—the signal for the other boys to act.

"There it is!" said James. He and the others raced across the clearing and grabbed the first canoe.

"The paddles!" James hissed at Ted, while he and Prentiss flipped the canoe over and hoisted it above their heads. The boys trotted off toward the lagoon as fast as they could while Ted followed, dragging four long paddles.

Thomas joined them, taking hold of the canoe in the middle.

"What did Fighting Prawn do to the girls?" asked

James, huffing from the effort of carrying the canoe.

"He sent them to their hut," huffed Thomas. Shining Pearl had expected this but had assured the boys that she and Little Scallop would escape quickly to join them at the lagoon.

"Ted," said James, "after you leave the paddles by the lagoon, head up onto those rocks. We'll watch for you. If you raise two hands over your head, that means the warriors are coming. Your two arms held out straight at your side means everything's okay, the coast is clear."

"Got it," huffed Ted. "But if the warriors *are* coming, what will you do about it?"

"We have to hope we've found Teacher by then," said James, "and brought the mermaids to their senses."

"But what if you haven't?" said Ted.

"We will," said James grimly, as the murky lagoon waters came into view. "We have to."

CHAPTER 9

BUBBLES RISING

THE CANOE LEFT THE BEACH BEHIND as it glided under the rocky cliff where Ted stood as lookout. In the distance ahead lay Mermaid Island, but the children's attention was focused on the water, as they watched anxiously for signs of mermaids.

Suddenly Little Scallop raised her arm and pointed. "Look!" she shouted.

A bubbling wake had broken the surface of the murky lagoon. It was heading right at the canoe.

"Brace yourself!" shouted Thomas, grabbing the canoe's edge. James and Prentiss raised their paddles, prepared to strike.

But just as the bubbling line was about to reach the canoe, the water exploded in front of it. The bubbles veered sharply to the right, away from the canoe.

"It's Ted!" said Little Scallop, pointing at rocky cliff. Ted waved down with his left hand; in his right he held a large rock. As the children watched, he took aim and heaved it. There was another big splash as the rock hit the lagoon just behind the trail of bubbles, which zoomed farther from the canoe.

"Ted's quite good at throwing, isn't he?" said Shining Pearl, impressed. "He nearly hit that mermaid."

The boys nodded. Prentiss said, "He learned that by flinging rocks to bring down coconuts. He's the best at that."

"He's protecting us," James said. "Paddle quickly."

The children dug their paddles into the water, and the canoe shot forward. Several more mermaids tried to approach, but each time they were driven away by well-aimed rocks thrown by Ted, who trotted along the cliff above to keep up.

The canoe was quickly approaching Mermaid Island. Ted, nearly out of range now, unleashed a volley of stones that splashed into the water around the canoe, except for one that thunked into the canoe hull.

"Sorry!" called Ted.

"We're all right!" James called back. "Nice work, Ted!"

On the cliff, Ted beamed with pride.

"Look!" said Shining Pearl. "There's Teacher!"

The mermaid leader was perched on a high rock next to the island. With her were three younger mermaids.

Shining Pearl waved at Teacher, expecting to get a wave and a smile in return. Instead Teacher's face remained grim. Instead of a wave, she raised her hand in an odd half salute.

"What was that?" said Prentiss.

"Maybe she wants us to go closer?" said Little Scallop.

James frowned. He looked around at the water near the canoe. "Do you think we should?" he said.

"Of course we should," said Shining Pearl. "We came out to talk to her, didn't we?"

"Yes," said James. "But she's acting odd. And those other mermaids back there were coming after us."

"But *Teacher's* not," countered Shining Pearl. "And Ted has driven the others off."

The canoe drifted forward a few more feet toward the island. Teacher and the three younger mermaids were still watching, unmoving, their faces blank.

"I don't like this," said James.

"Teacher!" Shining Pearl called. "We need to speak with you!"

A flicker of emotion crossed Teacher's face, but she said nothing. The canoe drifted closer.

"Please!" said Shining Pearl. "It's important."

No response from Teacher. The canoe kept drifting.

"I don't like this at *all*," said James. "Let's at least be ready to paddle."

"Good idea," said Prentiss. He, James, Prentiss, and Shining Pearl picked up their paddles and put them in the water.

Suddenly there was a shout from Ted on the cliff. "WATCH OUT!"

The children turned to look, and as they did, all four paddles were yanked violently out of their grips and pulled straight down into the murky lagoon. Gone.

"Let's get out of here!" shouted James. "Use your hands!"

He and James started to paddle with their hands, but quickly yanked them back out of the water to avoid being bitten by the needlelike teeth of the hissing mermaids who now surrounded the canoe.

On the cliff, Ted was shouting and hurling rock after rock as hard as he could, but it was no use; the canoe was out of range. The children could do nothing but hang on in terror as the canoe, propelled by the mermaids around them, shot toward the island and Teacher. As it reached the island, the right side was suddenly yanked under water, sending the children, screaming, into the lagoon. Hissing mermaids appeared from everywhere now, grabbing the children and dragging them onto the rocks just below where Teacher sat.

"Please!" Shining Pearl shouted at Teacher. "Please stop! We just want to talk to you! *Please.*"

For a moment, Shining Pearl thought she saw something in the mermaid leader's eyes. But Teacher said nothing. She stared down silently as the mermaids bound the children's hands behind their backs, using rope made of braided seaweed. They lay on the rocks, helpless, surrounded by snarling mermaids baring their sharp teeth.

"What are they going to do to us?" whispered Prentiss.

"I don't know," whispered James.

"We've got to get out of here," whispered Shining Pearl. "Father will be coming soon with the warriors to attack. If the mermaids see them coming, there's no telling what they'll do to us."

Little Scallop leaned over and buried her face in

her big sister's shoulder, sobbing. Shining Pearl looked at James and again whispered, "We've got to get out of here."

James nodded, looking at the ring of hostile she-fish surrounding them. They definitely had to get out of there.

But how?

CHAPTER 10

A STRATEGIC GENIUS

CAPTAIN HOOK STOOD ON THE TOP of the mountain ridge that ran along the center of Mollusk Island, dividing it into two. From here, he could look down the mountainside he had just climbed and see the pirate fort, which sat in a clearing far below. Looking down the other side of the mountain, Hook could see the Mollusk village, which sat in the flatland between the mountain and the sea.

Hook's sharp sailor's eyes scanned the rugged green mountainside leading down to the Mollusk village, until he found what he was looking for. He turned to Smee, sitting on the ground, puffing and red-faced from the climb.

"Smee," said Hook, pointing. "D'you see that?"

Smee heaved himself to his feet and squinted into the distance.

"The sea, Cap'n?" he said.

Hook sighed a deep sigh. "Smee," he said.

"What, Cap'n?"

"D'you really think," said Hook, his voice starting low but rising in volume, "that I would have us climb all the way up this mountain TO SHOW YOU THE SEA?"

Smee frowned, thinking about it. "I was wondering about that, Cap'n," he said. "Because there's sea on our side of the island, too. If you want, I can show you."

Hook started to clap his hand to his forehead, but stopped himself. The last time he'd clapped his hand to his forehead, he had forgetfully used the hand with the hook on it and given himself a nasty cut. So instead he rolled his eyes.

"Smee," he said.

"Cap'n?"

"You are an idjit."

"Aye, Cap'n."

"Actually, you are far stupider than an idjit, Smee. Calling you an idjit is an insult to idjits."

"Aye, Cap'n."

"Now," said Hook, "what I want you to do is very carefully look where I am pointing. I am not pointing at the sea, Smee. I am fully aware that, this being an island, I can see the sea in all directions. What I am pointing at, Smee, is the ravine that runs from the savages' village to a spot halfway up the side of the mountain. D'you see the ravine I mean, Smee?"

Smee squinted. "Aye, Cap'n," he said.

"Good," said Hook. "Now, follow that ravine up the mountain with your eye. D'you see where it ends, about halfway up?"

"Aye, Cap'n."

"And what do you see at that spot?"

"Smoke, Cap'n."

"Good, Smee. And where is that smoke coming from?"

"A lava pit, Cap'n."

"Correct, Smee!" said Hook. "And that is precisely what we need."

Smee frowned. "Cap'n," he said, "there's lava

pits on our side of the island, if we need one."

This was true: Mollusk Island was actively volcanic. There were a half-dozen places where lava bubbled up from the mountainside, forming bubbling, smoking cauldrons, some of which overflowed, sending rivers of hot lava down to the sea.

"I know that, Smee," said Hook. "But *this* lava pit is in the perfect spot for my plan to get us off this wretched island."

Smee frowned. "Beggin' the cap'n's pardon, but I don't see how—"

"Of *course* you don't," said Hook. "It takes a man of my strategic genius—" He tapped his forehead with his hand, making sure it was his non-hook hand. "—to think of a plan like this."

"Aye, Cap'n."

"Now, pay close attention," said Hook, who had been thinking about this for hours and was eager to exhibit his brilliance to *somebody*, even Smee. "What do we need to get off this wretched island?"

Smee frowned. "A ship?" he said.

"Good, Smee. A ship. Or a boat. Now, who, on this island, has boats?"

Smee frowned again. "The savages?"

"Excellent! So what we must do, if we are to get off the island, is take one of the savages' boats."

Smee looked concerned. "With all due respect, Cap'n," he said, "I don't think they'll let us."

"I *know* they won't let us, you idjit," said Hook. "That's why we're going to create a diversion."

"A what?" said Smee.

"A diversion. Something to distract them. And while they're paying attention to the diversion, we steal their boat."

"I see," said Smee.

"You do?" said Hook.

"No," said Smee.

Hook sighed. "The diversion," he said, "is lava. Flowing down that ravine straight toward the savage village, destroying everything in its path, and ultimately turning their village to ashes." Hook smiled at the thought.

Smee squinted down the mountain. "But Cap'n," he said, "that lava doesn't flow down the hill. It just bubbles and smells bad."

"That's all it does now," said Hook. "But we're going to change that with the keg."

"The what?" said Smee.

"The *gunpowder*, idjit."

"Ah!" said Smee, impressed. Smee himself had forgotten all about the keg.

"We blow out the side of the lava pit," said Hook. "The lava surges down the mountainside toward the village, destroying everything." Hook described this scene almost sadly, because he would not get to see it. "And while the savages are trying to save their village, we help ourselves to their biggest and finest boat. Maybe two boats. And by the time the savages realize what happened, we're far away."

Smee said nothing. He could only gaze in awe, overcome by his captain's brilliance. Hook saw the admiration in Smee's eyes and basked in it for a few moments. Then he turned and started down the mountainside toward the pirate fort.

"Let's go get that keg," he said, "and get off this wretched island."

CHAPTER 11

MOVEMENT ON THE MOUNTAINSIDE

TED WAS FRANTIC. He'd watched helplessly from the cliff as his friends had been captured by the mermaids and dragged behind some rocks out of his sight. He'd turned away from the cliff's edge and started running up Waterfall Hill, trying to get a better view. Every few steps he stopped, gasping for breath, and turned back to look for his friends. But they remained hidden from his sight.

As Ted struggled up the steep hillside, troubling thoughts tumbled around his brain. Why had the mermaids captured his friends? And what could he do about it? Should he tell Fighting Prawn? But wouldn't that make the chief even angrier and put his friends more at risk?

Sweat gushed down Ted's face as he climbed higher. He turned again to look toward Mermaid Island.

There!

Finally he could see over the rocks and just make out the heads of his friends. They were seated, facing Teacher, who was perched on a rock with several other mermaids. The canoe had been dragged behind the rocks, hidden from the beach.

Ted studied the scene for a minute. Nothing was happening; his friends appeared to be all right—for now. But what did the mermaids plan to do? And how would they react when the Mollusks attacked?

Ted cast a worried gaze to his right toward the Mollusk village. He saw no sign yet of the warriors, although he knew they could be keeping out of sight, approaching the lagoon under the cover of the jungle.

Then, suddenly, Ted saw movement on the mountainside high above the village. He shaded his eyes with his hand, straining to see. . . .

Pirates! They were coming down from the mountain ridge that divided the island. Ted frowned. This was very odd: the pirates *never* came to the Mollusk side of the island. He studied the line of pirates as they picked their way down the steep slope. There was Hook, in the lead, and behind him was a man carrying . . . Ted squinted to get a better look. . . .

The gunpowder keg! Ted watched the pirates for several minutes. There was no question: they were carrying the keg down toward the Mollusk village. But why? Ted wished more than anything that Peter was with him, or James, to help him figure out what the pirates were up to. Something bad—he was sure of that. He was also sure something should be done about it. But at the moment, there seemed to be nobody who could do it except Ted.

But what, exactly, *was* he supposed to do?

CHAPTER 12

TEACHER SPEAKS

THE FIVE CHILDREN SAT with their backs against the hard rocks, looking up at Teacher, who was perched above them. The children sat as still as they could; they were surrounded by mermaids who watched them closely, hissing and baring their sharp teeth at the slightest movement. Teacher, normally in total command of Mermaid Island, did nothing to stop this. She seemed to be as afraid of the other mermaids as the children were.

Shining Pearl thought Teacher looked sick. Her normally dark green tail was pale; her face looked tired, her eyes sunk deep in their sockets. As

Shining Pearl looked at Teacher, their gazes met, and, for the first time since the children had been captured, Teacher spoke.

"Are you all right?" she said, her voice cautious, almost a whisper.

Several of the mermaids hissed. Teacher looked at them, and Shining Pearl could tell she was talking to them without using words. This was how mermaids communicated; the children called it "eye-talking."

Turning back to Shining Pearl, Teacher again said, "Are you all right? Answer quietly and don't move."

Shining Pearl, darting her eyes toward the other mermaids, said, "They can't understand us?"

"Only I can speak English," Teacher said. "They have no idea what we're saying. And I'm still the one in charge . . . at least for now." She glanced around at the mermaid guards, who were listening with expressions of hostility and suspicion. "I don't know how much longer I can control them."

"But what's happening?" asked Shining Pearl. "Why are they attacking my people? Why did they capture us?"

"It's an illness," said Teacher. "A terrible disease. It has spread from one mermaid to another. It makes them angry and violent. They attack anything that swims or floats. They've even been attacking each other. I can control them some of the time, but it's getting harder. Several times I thought they were about to attack me."

"But what's making it happen?" asked Shining Pearl. "And why hasn't it affected you?"

"Because I was lucky enough to be out of the water when it started," said Teacher. "And when I realized what was happening, I stayed out of the water and avoided eating. I tried to tell the others, but it was too late."

James, who like the other children had been listening intently, said, "What's wrong with the water?"

Teacher nodded toward the lagoon. "Can't you see?"

The children looked out at the water.

"It's cloudier than usual," said James.

"Sort of reddish," said Thomas.

"We call it the Blood Tide," said Teacher. "We've seen it before in the warm months, but never in the

lagoon. It turns the sea red and harms whatever swims in it. We've always stayed away from it, but it caught us this time by coming into the lagoon."

"We've seen it, too," said Shining Pearl. "At least our fishermen have. It kills the fish and turtles. Birds too, sometimes. The fishermen never keep fish killed by the Blood Tide, because if people eat it, it makes them sick, too. But you're right—it never came into the lagoon before. Why is it here now?"

"I don't know," said Teacher. "I've been sitting here asking myself that same question. If the Blood Tide doesn't go away soon, I . . . I don't know what will happen. My mermaids are getting sicker, and I can't last much longer without going into the water or eating."

"I'm afraid that's not the only bad news," Shining Pearl said grimly.

"What do you mean?" said Teacher.

"Warriors are coming," said Shining Pearl.

"*What?*"

Shining Pearl told Teacher about her father's efforts to hold back his warriors, to make contact with Teacher, the attack on his canoe, and his decision to attack Mermaid Island.

"They're going to attack any minute," she concluded. "We came out to warn you about it."

"But, that's terrible!" said Teacher. "If only we could get word to him, explain about the Blood Tide sickness. . . ."

"Ted's back on the island," said James. "Maybe we could signal him somehow."

The children turned to look back over the rocks. The mermaid guards hissed at the movement, but Teacher was able to quiet them.

"I think I see Ted!" said Little Scallop. "He's way up high above the cliff on Waterfall Hill!"

Teacher and the children looked up the hill and, one by one, spotted the tiny figure of Ted.

"I don't know how we can signal him," said James. "If we yell, these mermaids are likely to attack us." Indeed, the mermaids were edging closer, hissing, clearly unhappy with all the conversation.

"Hold on," said Prentiss, his eyes on the hill. "Where's the waterfall?"

"What?" said Shining Pearl.

"The waterfall," said Prentiss. "On Waterfall Hill. Where is it?"

The rest of them looked and then gasped.

Prentiss was right. The waterfall that gave the hill its name, which usually splashed into the lagoon from the cliff's edge, wasn't there.

"I don't understand," said Little Scallop. "How could a waterfall be missing?"

"The earthquake!" said James. "It must have shifted the stream that fed the waterfall!"

Shining Pearl frowned at the lagoon. "That must be what caused the Blood Tide," she said. "There's no freshwater coming into the lagoon."

"If that's true," said Teacher, "the mermaids—all of us—are doomed."

"No!" said Shining Pearl. "Maybe my father can fix it! If I can just explain to him . . ."

"But how?" said James. "We're trapped out here."

"And your father's about to attack," said Thomas.

"I've got to get ashore somehow," said Shining Pearl. "Teacher, can you think of a way?"

Teacher glanced at the shore, then the captured children, then the surrounding mermaid guards.

"Perhaps," she said. "But it will be dangerous."

"Tell us what to do," said Shining Pearl. The other children nodded.

"All right," she said. "I'm about to talk with these

mermaids in a way that will distract them. While I'm doing that, I want you to quietly untie each other's hands. Try not to move too much and keep your hands behind you. Are you ready?"

The children nodded.

"Then do it now," said Teacher. She turned to the mermaids and quickly had their attention. While they stared at Teacher's eyes, the children worked each other free of their seaweed ropes. After a minute Teacher turned back to them.

"Are you ready?" she said.

The children nodded.

"Good. Now comes the difficult part. Shining Pearl, you and Prentiss are going to swim for shore."

"Why them?" said James. "Thomas and I can—"

"Because they are closest to the water," said Teacher. "And because Fighting Prawn is most likely to listen to his daughter. And I need the rest of you—" She nodded at James, Thomas, and Little Scallop. "—to create a diversion. But I warn you, this next part is a bit dangerous."

"We're not afraid," said Little Scallop. The rest nodded in agreement, although they were all, in fact, afraid.

"All right then," said Teacher. "Listen very carefully. In a moment, I will make a loud warning sound. This will signal to the mermaids that an attack is coming. They will look back toward the beach. When they do, the three of you—" She nodded to James, Thomas, and Little Scallop. "—must grab the canoe and pull it up on Mermaid Island as fast as you can. Drag across until you're on the other side, out of sight. Then launch it into the water, but do not get into it. Instead, hide in the bushes."

"Why shouldn't we get into the canoe?" said Thomas.

"Because the mermaids would catch you. I want them to see the canoe and chase after it. When they find it, I want you to come out from the bushes, waving your arms and shouting, so they see you're still on Mermaid Island. Then they'll come back here after you. And while that's going on—" She turned to Shining Pearl and Prentiss. "—swim back to the beach as fast as you can. Does everybody understand?"

"What happens if the mermaids catch us while we're being a diversion?" said Little Scallop.

"You'll have the advantage, at least for a while,"

said Teacher. "They don't move well on the land. Mermaid Island is small, but if you stay away from the water, you should be able to avoid them until help comes."

"*If* help comes," said James, thinking about being pursued around this small, rocky bit of land by a group of angry, sharp-toothed mermaids.

"It will come," said Shining Pearl. "We'll get help. I promise."

James nodded, but he didn't look convinced.

"All right then," said Teacher. "Get ready." With a sudden movement, she raised up on her rock perch and made a terrifyingly loud shrieking sound, pointing toward the lagoon beach. Instantly the other mermaids whirled to look, clambering across the rocks toward the water.

"Now!" said Teacher. "The canoe!"

James, Thomas, and Little Scallop leaped to their feet, ran to the canoe, and grabbed it. In seconds they were dragging it up the rocks and across the little island. It was a few more seconds before one of the mermaids spotted them. She made a shrieking sound like the one Teacher had made. The other mermaids whirled to see the children disappearing over the top of the island with the canoe. At once the mermaids were in the water, splashing their huge, powerful tails as they shot around the island to intercept the children on the other side. From her perch, Teacher watched them go. She looked down at Shining Pearl and Prentiss.

"Go!" she whispered. "Swim as fast as you can and *don't look back*."

A second later, Shining Pearl and Prentiss plunged into the warm, murky lagoon water, swimming for the beach as hard as they could, each one fearing that at any moment the mad mermaids would see them and hunt them down.

CHAPTER 13

ESCAPE

SHINING PEARL SWAM with all her strength. She was a graceful swimmer and a good deal faster than Prentiss. Despite Teacher's instruction not to look back, she glanced behind her. She saw Prentiss flailing in her wake, but she saw no mermaids coming. So far, Teacher's plan was working.

She turned and swam some more. With each breath she looked ahead. The lagoon beach, she realized, was farther than it had appeared to be. On and on she swam. She was starting to tire, her lungs aching, her muscles cramping. She turned back; Prentiss, clearly exhausted, had fallen farther behind her. She glanced again back toward the island.

Oh, no.

The mermaids had figured out the ruse. Several were up on the rocks, shrieking and pointing toward Shining Pearl and Prentiss. A half-dozen powerful green tails splashed the water.

The mermaids were coming.

Shining Pearl, starting to panic, looked ahead. The beach, on an angle to her left, was probably too far away to reach in time. Directly ahead was a small rocky cove; ordinarily, this was where the waterfall splashed into the lagoon after falling down the side of the steep cliff. They'd have to aim for that instead of the beach.

"Prentiss!" she gasped. He looked up, his face fearful and tired. Shining Pearl pointed toward the waterfall cove. "That way!" she shouted.

He nodded and changed course. Shining Pearl looked behind him and saw the lagoon surface rippling with the fast-moving V-shaped trails of the oncoming mermaids. She waited until Prentiss had caught up, then swam next to him.

"Hurry!" she urged. But she could see he wasn't

nearly fast enough. Neither was she. The ripples were closing fast. The shore was too far away. The mermaids were going to catch them. She let Prentiss get ahead and fell directly behind him. She glanced back; the ripples were almost upon them. Shining Pearl drew her feet up, preparing to kick back hard the instant she felt a bite. Suddenly she heard a splash; she let out an involuntary scream as something broke the surface next to her. She balled her fist and turned, ready to punch. . . .

Ammm!

The sight of the dolphin's familiar, smiling snout filled her with relief. He was chittering rapidly, but

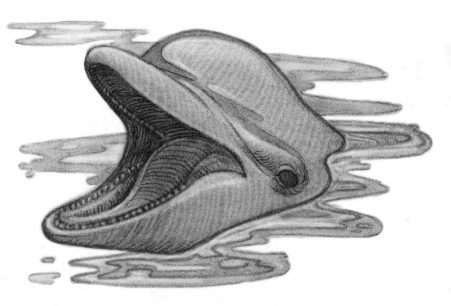

Shining Pearl didn't understand him; unlike Ammm's old friends Peter and Molly, Shining Pearl did not speak porpoise. She immediately understood, however, what Ammm wanted her to do. She grabbed hold of his dorsal fin and held on tight as he surged forward, a half second before the closest pursuing mermaid burst from the lagoon, her razor teeth snapping at the air where Shining Pearl had just been. Ammm sped ahead and Shining Pearl, hanging on to his fin with her left hand, reached out with her right to grab Prentiss' arm. Now all three shot forward, Shining Pearl and Prentiss hanging on, literally, for dear life. Ammm was a very powerful swimmer, but the weight of the children slowed him greatly; he was barely able to keep ahead of the pursing mermaids. He headed for the closest land—the waterfall cove. They reached it five seconds ahead of the mermaids—just enough time for Shining Pearl and Prentiss to scramble from the water and onto the rocks at the base of the waterfall. Shining Pearl yelled her thanks to Ammm, but the porpoise had spun and shot away, clearly not wanting to fall into the mermaids' clutches.

For the moment, Shining Pearl and Prentiss were safe. But only for the moment. The walls of the waterfall cove rose almost straight up from the lagoon on both sides. They couldn't get back to the lagoon beach without going back into the water, which was filled with hissing, snarling mermaids. Some of the mermaids were starting to climb up the rocks toward the children. Prentiss was watching them anxiously.

"What are we going to do?" he said.

Shining Pearl looked around. There was only one way out.

"We're going to have to climb the cliff," she said.

Prentiss looked at the towering, vertical rock wall behind them.

"But how?" he said. "We'll never get up that!"

"It's either that," said Shining Pearl, "or we wait for the mermaids to get us."

Prentiss looked at the cliff, the mermaids, and the cliff again.

"All right then," he said. "Let's go."

CHAPTER 14

DEVIL'S HOLE

FOR SEVERAL MINUTES, Ted had watched as the pirates made their way down from the mountain ridge. He was pretty sure now where they were going: a place the Mollusks called by a name that, in English, would be something like "Devil's Hole."

Shining Pearl had taken the boys to see Devil's Hole once: it was a lava-filled pit on a level place in the mountainside that belched steam and stinky sulfur fumes. Shining Pearl said that generations ago, the lava spilled out and flowed down to the village, causing terrible destruction. Eventually the flow stopped, and the Mollusks built a stone wall in hopes of diverting any future flow. But they kept a wary eye on the smoking, steaming hole on the hillside.

Ted wondered why the pirates were heading toward Devil's Hole and why they had brought the keg. He was about to creep closer to spy on them when he heard somebody yell, "Help!"

The yell came from the direction of the lagoon. Ted ran down the hill until he came to the cliff. Ted was not fond of heights, so he got down on hands and knees and crept forward until he could look over the edge of the steep cliff. He was shocked to see Shining Pearl and Prentiss, who had somehow gotten off Mermaid Island, halfway up the cliff's side, both looking quite terrified. They had good reason to be, Ted saw. Not only were they clinging to a rock wall that was nearly straight up and down, but in the lagoon directly beneath them were some very angry mermaids.

"Up here!" Ted shouted.

"We're stuck!" Prentiss called back. "You've got to help us."

Ted saw the problem: Prentiss and Shining Pearl had reached a smooth, vertical part of the cliff. They couldn't climb any higher; there was nothing to grab

on to. They certainly couldn't go back down. And there was no way Ted could climb down to help them; he was dizzy just looking over the edge.

"Hang on!" he shouted. He crawled away from the cliff's edge, stood up, got rid of the dizzies, and looked around frantically. He was surrounded by rock; no help there. But off to his left he spotted a place where an outcropping of the cliff jutted over the jungle and a few tall trees poked their tops just above the cliff's edge. In those treetops, Ted hoped, were vines.

Ted ran to the outcropping and again dropped to his hands and knees to approach the edge next to one of the trees. The tree did, indeed, have vines, and nice thick ones at that. But the nearest vine was still several feet from the cliff's edge. To reach it, Ted would have to lean far out from the cliff over empty air. He took a breath and closed his eyes, so he couldn't see the rocks at the base of the cliff at least one hundred feet straight down. He waved his hand around, fighting the dizziness growing inside him. Finally he caught a vine. He grabbed it and pulled, but the vine resisted him, clinging to the tree branch. He was very dizzy now; he was afraid he'd lose his balance and plunge to the rocks below. With a desperate heave, he jerked the vine. He heard the leaves rustle as the vine parted reluctantly from the branch, and then he fell backward onto solid ground. From here he could get more traction, and with effort he pulled a twenty-foot length of vine from the tree. But twenty feet was not enough. Twice more Ted had to force himself to lean out over the cliff to get vines; the second one was so far away that Ted very nearly lost his balance. When he finally got that vine, he lay on the rocks for a full minute, waiting for his pounding heart to settle down.

Then he rose and carefully and tied the three vines together, using knots that the boys had been taught by the Mollusks. He hoped the combined vines would be long enough. They would have to be.

Ted coiled the vines and ran back to the top of the dry waterfall. He leaned over—it didn't seem so scary now after what he'd done to get the vines—and was relieved to see that Prentiss and Shining Pearl were where he'd left them.

"Hullo!" he shouted down. They looked up, and Ted saw the exhaustion and fear on their faces.

"I'm going to lower a vine!" he shouted. Prentiss

and Shining Pearl nodded. Ted made a noose on one end of the vine and draped it over a large boulder. He then wrapped a loop around his waist and tossed the other end of the vine over the cliff. He didn't dare get close to the edge to see what was happening, but he saw the vine grow taut, so he knew somebody had grabbed hold of it. He prayed that the vine was strong enough and that his knots would hold. He leaned back, using his weight to steady the vine. He felt somebody climbing, then resting, then climbing some more. It took several minutes—it seemed to Ted like an hour—but finally he saw a hand reach the top of the cliff, and then Shining Pearl's face, wet with sweat. He grabbed her and helped her scramble to safety.

"Thank you," she gasped. She lay on the rock, panting, while Ted heaved the vine back over the edge. In a few minutes Prentiss, too, was safe.

"Good work, Ted," Prentiss said, when he'd caught his breath. "I thought we were done for."

"How'd you get off Mermaid Island?" said Ted. "And what happened to the others?"

Quickly, Prentiss and Shining Pearl told Ted about their escape and about the Blood Tide.

"We've got to get to my father," said Shining Pearl. "We need to explain about the sickness before the warriors attack the mermaids."

"There's something else we need to tell him," said Ted. "The pirates are up to something." He told them about seeing Hook and his men on the mountainside nearby.

"But why would they be going to Devil's Hole?" said Prentiss.

"And why are they taking the gunpowder?" added Ted.

"Whatever Hook is planning," said Shining Pearl, "I suspect it's not good. Listen, we have to head toward Devil's Hole to get to my father, anyway. Maybe on the way we can see what the pirates are up to."

Moments later they were heading up Waterfall Hill, keeping hidden from view by walking in the bed carved by the now-dry stream. They'd gone fifty yards when they came to a huge mound of recently disturbed earth and rock, completely blocking the streambed.

"So that's what stopped the waterfall," said Prentiss. "The earthquake must have done this.

They climbed up onto the mound and found, on the other side, a large pond formed by the backed-up stream water. The overflow, unable to follow the stream's usual course, flowed out off to the side, creating a new stream that went down a different side of Waterfall Hill.

"That water's going to the sea now," said Shining Pearl. "It can't reach the lagoon. That's what caused the Blood Tide."

"If we could move this dirt," said Prentiss, "the stream would go back into the lagoon."

"Oh, right," said Ted, looking at the massive mound of dirt and huge rocks. "Go ahead and move this, would you please, Prentiss?"

"I'm not saying it would be easy," said Prentiss.

"Easy? How about *impossible?*" said Ted.

"I suppose you're right," said Prentiss. He turned to Shining Pearl. "We'd better get going, then, if we're going to tell your father about the mermaids and the pirates."

At those words, Shining Pearl, who'd been staring at the earth mound, snapped her head around.

"But that's *it*," she said.

"What's it?" said Prentiss.

Instead of answering, Shining Pearl turned to Ted and said, "Which way are the pirates?"

CHAPTER 15

THE CHIEF'S CLEVER PLAN

FIGHTING PRAWN LEANED on his spear, which he had stuck into the earth where the dirt of the jungle met the sand of the lagoon.

He looked out toward Mermaid Island and then shifted his eyes toward a distant curve of beach, over a half mile away, where some mermaids had gathered. They were next to the place where the steep cliff began; past that, out of sight, was the cove formed by the now-absent waterfall. Fighting Prawn had been watching the mermaids for a while, wondering what they were up to. He knew they were watching him, too; mermaids had very good eyes.

He looked back toward the jungle. His warriors were laboring to carry twelve large, heavy dugout canoes overland from the oceanside beach to the lagoon, in preparation for the attack on Mermaid Island. Other Mollusks were carrying coils of rope woven from vines and elephant grass. In fact, it seemed as if the whole village had come to the lagoon to watch the battle.

When the canoes were in the shallow water by the beach, Fighting Prawn ordered the men to arrange them in three groups of four canoes each.

"Now," said Fighting Prawn, "lash the canoes together, side by side." The men looked puzzled; this wasn't how they launched canoes. Fighting Prawn, raising his voice, said, "The mermaids are strong enough to flip a single canoe. But they can't flip four canoes if we lash them together, as we do when we are caught at sea in a storm."

The men smiled at their chief's cleverness. But Fighting Prawn did not smile. He was troubled by the mermaids at the end of the lagoon. Something else troubled him as well. His eyes scanned the tribe, and he frowned. He called over his eldest son, Bold Abalone, and spoke to him softly.

"I don't see Shining Pearl or Little Scallop," he said.

"You sent them to the hut," reminded Bold Abalone.

"I know that," said Fighting Prawn, "but I also know my daughters. They wouldn't stay in the village with this excitement going on."

"Do you want me to look for them?" said Bold Abalone.

Fighting Prawn looked at the canoes; his men had finished lashing them together into rafts. "No," he told Bold Abalone. "I need you here." He turned to his warriors and ordered them to ready the rafts. He grabbed his spear and climbed onto the first raft. As the men pushed it into the lagoon and began paddling, he turned his gaze toward Mermaid Island and the mermaids watching him from the end of the lagoon. He tried to concentrate his thoughts on the battle ahead. But he couldn't rid his mind of a lingering worry.

Where were his daughters?

CHAPTER 16

THE CHILDREN GROW WEARY

"WHAT ARE WE GOING TO DO?" said Little Scallop, her voice quavering with fear, her eyes on the hissing, snarling mermaids crawling toward them.

"We've got to keep moving," said James, trying to keep the fear out of his own voice. "It's all we can do."

"What happens when we're too tired to move?" asked Thomas.

James had no answer for that. The mermaids were in fact getting closer. It had taken them only a few minutes to flip the decoy canoe and discover it was empty; they had soon spotted Little Scallop, James, and Thomas hiding behind some rocks on Mermaid Island. Since then the mermaids had been relentlessly pursuing the children around the island.

The children's legs gave them a temporary advantage; they were good climbers, and they could move quickly, keeping boulders between themselves and their pursuers. The mermaids had to use their arms to move on the land, dragging their long tails behind them. They had trouble climbing. But they could still move surprisingly quickly when they wanted to. They were starting to figure out that they could spread out, giving the children fewer places to hide. And time was working for them: the children were growing weary.

James had hoped that Teacher would protect them, but she was still on the high rock, surrounded by mermaids who now were clearly holding her prisoner. She could not help the children, and they could not run forever. James looked toward Waterfall Hill but saw no sign of Ted, Prentiss, or Little Scallop. He saw no help coming from anywhere.

Meanwhile the mermaids, baring their sharp teeth, were getting closer and closer.

CHAPTER 17

THERE WON'T BE NOTHING LEFT

Ted led shining pearl and Prentiss off Waterfall Hill into the jungle. There they joined a path heading down the steep mountainside toward Devil's Hole. They moved as quietly as they could, not wanting the pirates to hear them coming. In a few minutes they heard men's voices ahead. Ted raised his hand, and they all stopped to listen. The first words they could make out were in the snarling voice of Captain Hook.

"That's the spirit, men," he said. "There won't be nothing left of them savages by the time we're through!"

The children looked at each other in horror. Shining Pearl moved close to the two boys and whispered, "Through with *what*? What are they doing?"

"Let's find out," whispered Prentiss. The three children stepped off the path and crept through the thick jungle toward the pirates. They stopped on a ledge above Devil's Hole. The air reeked of sulfur. Carefully parting the curtain of green plants, the children peered down at the scene below.

Almost directly underneath was Devil's Hole, which belched steam and glowed red from the bubbling lava inside. Just beyond was the stone wall built by the Mollusks to protect their village. On the

slope beyond the wall stood Hook, Smee, and the rest of the pirates. The gunpowder keg stood nearby on a level spot of ground. Two of the pirates, using tree limbs as crude shovels, were digging a hole at the base of the wall. The men stopped for a moment to wipe the sweat from their foreheads.

"Cap'n," said one, "is this deep enough?"

Hook stepped forward, bent, and peered into the hole with his glittering black eyes. He stood back up, raised his left arm—the twisted question mark of a hook glinting in the sun—and carefully scratched his cheek with its sharpened point.

"A bit deeper," he said. "We have only the one keg. We'd best be sure we blow a nice big hole in the wall."

The men looked unhappy but were not about to question Captain Hook. They resumed digging.

"Cap'n?" said Smee.

"What is it, Smee?" said Hook.

"How are you planning to light the powder when the time comes? We ain't got no fire up here."

Hook smiled. He had already thought about this problem—yet more proof of his brilliance. "We have plenty of fire, Smee," he said.

"We do?" said Smee.

"We do," said Hook. "Right down that hole there." He pointed his hook hand toward the steaming lava pit. "When I give the signal, you'll stick the end of a tree branch into that lava there, and it'll burst right into flames. Then you'll drop the burning branch into the hole with the powder. She'll blow quite nicely."

Smee frowned, thinking. After a few moments, he said. "Cap'n?"

"What, Smee?"

"When you say I'm going to light the powder, do you mean . . . *I'm* going to light the powder?"

"Yes," said Hook. "I'd do it myself, of course, but I need to supervise the stealing of the savages' boat. So you'll blow the powder, then come down to join us, taking care to avoid the lava flow."

Smee's frown deepened. "But, Cap'n," he said. "Ain't it a bit dangerous? Being right here when the powder blows, I mean? And the lava coming down the mountain?"

"Not at all, Smee!" said Hook. "You'll have several, er, moments to get away. I'm sure it's perfectly safe, which is why I've chosen you, as first mate, for the honor."

Smee looked very doubtful about this honor, but

Hook turned away to inspect the diggers' progress with the hole.

"Another foot, men," he said. "Then we'll put the keg inside and get ready to blow this wall." He looked down at Mollusk Village, at the foot of the ravine leading from Devil's Hole down the mountainside. "We'll be saying good-bye to this cursed island," he said. "And them savages will be saying good-bye to their village."

On the ledge above Devil's Hole, Shining Pearl, Prentiss, and Ted crawled back into the jungle and up the mountainside, out of earshot from the pirates.

"They're going to blow up the wall!" said Ted.

"And destroy the village with lava!" said Prentiss.

"Just to steal a *boat*," said Shining Pearl, bitterly. "I've got to tell father *now*."

"It may be a little late for that," said Ted.

"What do you mean?" said Shining Pearl.

"Look," said Ted, pointing to an open space between two trees through which the lagoon could be seen far below. Shining Pearl and Prentiss looked and gasped when they saw what Ted had seen. A large raft made of canoes lashed together had pushed off from the shore. Dozens of warriors were aboard, paddling hard toward Mermaid Island. At the front of the raft stood a tall figure holding a spear. Shining Pearl couldn't make out his face at this distance, but there was no doubt in her mind who it was.

Fighting Prawn had launched the attack.

CHAPTER 18

THE WATER TURNS WHITE

THE BULKY CANOE RAFT MOVED SLOWLY across the lagoon, paddled by two-dozen sweating warriors. Another dozen stood ready with spears, their eyes on the murky water, watching for a mermaid attack.

At the front of the raft stood Fighting Prawn, his hand on his spear, his gaze aimed straight ahead at Mermaid Island. He could see a lot of activity; there were mermaids moving along the island's rocky shore, watching the raft. Others were crawling around on the higher part of the island, as if chasing something, although Fighting Prawn could not see what.

As the raft drew closer, the mermaids on the shore became more agitated, their long green tails flicking back and forth, sparkling in the sunlight. Then one of them made a strange noise, loud and hoarse. Suddenly, with movements so quick that Fighting Prawn could barely follow them, they dove into the lagoon. For a few moments the water churned white, whipped by a dozen or more powerful tails. Then there was nothing. Fighting Prawn's eyes scanned the lagoon, but the water was flat—not a ripple, not a bubble.

Fighting Prawn turned to his men.

"Be ready," he said. "Paddlers, don't let them pull you in."

The men nodded. Fighting Prawn raised his face toward the sky and, as Mollusks had always done when going into battle, let out a war cry. The other men echoed him, their cry floating across the lagoon and echoing off the stark rock face of Waterfall Hill. It was an impressive sound, one that usually struck fear into the hearts of the enemy. But this enemy could not hear them. This enemy was invisible, silent. There was no way to know when, or how, they would attack.

Fighting Prawn glanced back. The raft had seemed big enough when they had launched it; it didn't seem so big now, away from the safety of land. He turned forward again, not wanting his men to see even a hint of concern on his face. He looked again at the water. He saw nothing. He gripped his spear tighter.

The attack was coming.

But when?

And from where?

CHAPTER 19

ROLLING
BOULDERS

J AMES CROUCHED BEHIND A ROCK, breathing hard, grateful for a moment's rest.

But then he heard it again, the sound he'd learned to fear—the sound of mermaids hissing and of their long tails dragging across the rocks, getting closer.

James, Little Scallop, and Thomas had decided to separate, hoping to make it harder for the mermaids to trap them. The children had spread out, each taking a different route, moving from rock to rock, heading for what little higher ground there was on the tiny island. James caught a few glimpses of Little

Scallop, but he'd lost sight of Thomas. He had little time to look around; each time he stopped, the mermaids got closer.

He heard them now just on the other side of his rock. He jumped up and ran farther up the hill. He was near the crest now; beyond that, there was no higher ground to escape to. He ducked behind another boulder, knowing it would not protect him for long. He leaned against it, growing weary.

The boulder moved. He leaned on it harder, and this time it rocked considerably forward, then back.

He peered around the side. Four mermaids were coming up the hill. The one in front caught sight of him, her eyes wild with fury. She hissed and bared her sharp teeth. She was only about twenty feet away. James shifted a few feet to his left to take a better angle.

He leaned hard against the boulder, tipping it forward. He let it rock back, then leaned on it again, then let it rock back. The mermaids were getting close. With a grunt, James heaved himself into the boulder again, rocking it still farther forward but not quite enough. He jumped back as the boulder came toward him. He heard hisses from the other side. As

the boulder rocked forward he hurled himself at it, putting all of his weight into it this time. The boulder almost stopped, but then broke free and rolled forward, straight toward the mermaid. She let out a horrifying screech, flipped herself backward down the hill and sideways, just barely avoiding the boulder as it tumbled past her and the other mermaids, rolling all the way down and splashing into the lagoon.

"Well done, James!"

James turned and saw Thomas running toward him, followed by Little Scallop. They, too, had been driven to the top of the hill, both followed closely by packs of mermaids. The three children quickly found other suitable boulders and, working together, were able to roll them down the hill in various directions, forcing their pursuers to retreat. But each time, after the boulders passed, the mermaids resumed dragging themselves upward toward their prey. And as the children used up the loose boulders, they found fewer and fewer that they could budge. With each passing minute, the mermaids were getting closer.

And then the children heard an awful sound:

hissing from *behind* them. They turned and saw more mermaids cresting the hill, coming at them from the other side of the island. Boulders would do no good against these pursuers: they were uphill from the children.

James, Thomas, and Little Scallop whirled back around and saw that the mermaids had now spread out along the hillside, dragging themselves steadily closer. The children had no way to get down on this side, and moving farther up the hill would only bring them closer to the other group of mermaids.

They were trapped.

CHAPTER 20

IT MIGHT HOLD A PIG

PRENTISS, TED, AND SHINING PEARL were running out of time. Below them, through the jungle plants, they could see that the pirates were almost finished digging the hole for the gunpowder keg. If the children didn't stop them, the pirates would soon blow up the wall, release the lava, and destroy the Mollusk village.

But how could three children stop a band of pirates? Prentiss looked around the jungle hillside, trying to come up with a plan. He wished Peter were here. Peter always knew what to do.

As he thought of Peter, something caught his eye.

Two things, actually: a mango tree about twenty yards away and, beneath it, a patch of brown leaves on the jungle floor.

"That's it!" he whispered.

"What is?" said Ted.

Prentiss pointed to the brown leaves and whispered to Shining Pearl, "That's a trap, right?"

She nodded and said, "The hunters use it to catch wild pigs. The pigs come to eat the mangos, and they fall in. There's a hole under the leaves about six feet deep."

"Maybe we can use it to catch some pirates," said Prentiss.

"A six-foot hole might hold a pig," said Ted, "but it won't hold a pirate."

"No, but it'll slow 'em down," said Prentiss.

"Maybe long enough for the two of us to grab that powder keg," said Shining Pearl.

"Us?" said Ted. "Me?"

Shining Pearl nodded. "It's the key to my plan."

"Then I'm not sure I like your plan," Ted said.

"You two hide here," said Prentiss. "I'll climb the mango tree and get Hook's attention the way Peter does."

When Peter was on the island, he greatly enjoyed flying over the pirate camp and bombarding Hook with juicy mangoes. This was yet another reason why Hook absolutely hated the flying boy.

"You're going to throw mangoes at Hook?" said Ted.

"Yes," said Prentiss. "I'm good at throwing."

"You'll be good and dead when the pirates come after you," said Ted.

Prentiss waved his hand. "They won't catch me," he said. "But while they're chasing me, you two will get the powder keg. Remember: we need it up on Waterfall Hill. I'll catch up to you when I get away from the pirates."

"*If* you get away," said Ted.

"I'll be fine," said Prentiss. "Just you take care of—"

"The gunpowder," said Shining Pearl. "Don't worry. We will!"

Ted looked doubtful, but he didn't have a better idea.

Leaving them, Prentiss crept quietly through the jungle toward the mango tree, steering clear of the pig trap. Shining Pearl led Ted in the other direction to a bush as close as she dared get to the pirates. She peered through the branches and saw that the pirates had finished digging the hole.

"All right, men," said Hook. "Bring that keg here and—"

Splat!

A large, overripe mango exploded at Hook's feet, spattering his legs with sticky pulp. Hook looked down at it for a moment, then looked up, his face darkening with rage. His glittering dark eyes scanned the jungle treetops.

Splat! A second mango burst on Hook's tattered pants. He roared in fury. It was that cursed flying boy again; he was sure of it.

"Boy?" he shouted, slipping the flintlock pistol from his waist, pulling back its hammer, and aiming it at the treetops.

When Ted saw the pistol, his face went white. Hook's pistol was usually just for show, because he had nothing to load it with. But now he had gunpowder—a whole keg of it. His pistol could actually shoot. Ted was about to shout a warning to Prentiss when a third mango hurtled through the air and hit Hook smack in the face, causing him to flinch just as he pulled the trigger. The flintlock discharged with a *bang* but was now aimed not at the trees, but at the broad backside of First Mate Smee, who yelped and leaped into the air higher than he had ever leaped before. Fortunately, Hook had no bullets for his gun, and thus had packed it with coral fragments. So Smee was not seriously wounded. But he was stung. He danced around, yipping as though his pants were on fire.

Meanwhile Hook was wiping the mango from his furious face, reloading his pistol, and bellowing orders to his men. "AFTER HIM!" he shouted, pointing uphill toward the jungle. "GET THAT CURSED FLYING MANGO-FLINGING BOY!"

The pirates charged up the hill, even Smee, who brought up the rear while holding his own with both hands.

The moment the pirates entered the jungle, Shining Pearl and Ted came out from behind the bush and ran to the gunpowder keg. It was heavier than it looked, so they put it on its side and, working together, began rolling it across the mountainside in the direction of Waterfall Hill.

Back in the tree, Prentiss had three more mangoes at his disposal. He took careful aim at the approaching pirates and managed to hit Hook with two of the three. In doing so, Prentiss also revealed his location.

"HE'S IN THAT TREE!" Hook bellowed, waving his pistol. "Hard to starboard, men!"

The pirates swung to their right and headed at a full run straight for the tree. Their path took them directly over the patch of brown leaves. The first man went down like a stone; the others, unable to stop in time, fell right in after him, one atop one another, with Hook and Smee last.

As the pirates roared in pain and surprise, Prentiss hung from a branch, dropped lightly to the jungle floor, and took off at a dead run. Meanwhile Hook was fighting his way out of the pig trap, using his hook to stab the ground and haul himself up while climbing on his men, as though they were rungs on a human ladder. As he sprawled out onto the jungle floor, he caught a glimpse of a boy escaping into the distance. . . .

On foot.

Hook roared in rage as he realized that it wasn't the flying boy. He'd been tricked. He was about to order his men to pursue the boy when he suddenly realized *why* he'd been tricked.

"The powder!" he roared, kicking at his men as they scrambled from the pit. "GET BACK TO THE POWDER!"

The pirates hurried back to Devil's Hole.

The keg was gone.

Hook whirled around, looking for the thieves.

"There!" he shouted, pointing across the

mountainside to two small figures in the distance, rolling the keg. As he watched, a third child joined them: the boy who had thrown the mangoes.

"AFTER THEM!" he screamed.

The pirates took off running toward the distant figures. Hook expected the children to head down toward the sea. But instead, as they reached the rocky ridge leading up to Waterfall Hill, they began to roll it *up* the hillside.

Hook smiled at their foolishness: once they were up that hill, there was nowhere for them to go.

"Hurry, men!" he shouted. "We've got them now!"

CHAPTER 21

THE BATTLE RAGED

THE ATTACK ON THE CANOE RAFT came from all sides at once. Fighting Prawn was lucky: he'd decided to crouch in the prow of his canoe, so he could get a better view into the water. Just as he bent his knees, a mermaid burst straight up out of the lagoon, her razor-sharp teeth snapping the air where his head had been. She grabbed at Fighting Prawn as she fell, trying to pull him with her into the water. He lunged backward, avoiding her but knocking over another warrior as he fell back into the canoe.

Struggling back up, he heard sounds of fighting

everywhere—the hissing of mermaids and shouts of rage and pain from his men. The mermaids were attacking from all sides, four or five of them at once, grabbing the paddles, sometimes using their teeth and astonishingly powerful jaws to snap them in two. The men tried to fight back with their spears, but the mermaids yanked and pulled at the raft, using their powerful tails to toss and turn it so that the warriors could not keep their balance. One of the warriors thrust his spear at a mermaid, who dodged sideways and grabbed the shaft, almost dragging the warrior into the water before he was forced to let go. Another warrior, trying to stand so he could use his spear, tumbled into the lagoon. Two mermaids lunged for him, but he was saved by two warriors who pulled him back onto the raft while two others drove the attackers back by smacking them with their paddles.

Meanwhile, no one was rowing. As the battle raged, Fighting Prawn noticed that the mermaids on the right-hand side of the raft were pushing it, while the mermaids on the other sides were not. Suddenly he realized that they had a plan—they were moving the raft away from Mermaid Island and toward the rocks at the base of Waterfall Hill, about fifty yards to his left. They were picking up speed; in a few minutes the raft would wreck against those rocks.

When it did, Fighting Prawn and his warriors would spill into the water, where their spears and their courage would be no match for the mermaids and their needlelike teeth.

CHAPTER 22

BOWLING FOR PIRATES

SHINING PEARL, TED, AND PRENTISS struggled to roll the powder keg up the steep and rocky slope of Waterfall Hill. It was slow going: the keg was heavier than it looked.

Shining Pearl glanced back over her shoulder at the pursuing pirates.

"We have to go faster!" she panted. "They're getting closer!"

Prentiss and Ted looked back and saw that the pirates, with Hook urging them on, were indeed much nearer than before. The three children turned and pushed the keg even harder. But each time they looked back, they saw the same troubling sight: the pirates were gaining.

The children were about fifty yards from the earth dam that had blocked the stream near the top of Waterfall Hill. It might as well have been a mile; they weren't going to outrun the pirates.

"They're going to catch us," panted Ted.

Prentiss looked around. To the left was a rock outcropping, and next to it swayed the green tops of some tall palm trees, rising up from the jungle below.

"Keep going!" Prentiss said. "I'll slow them down."

"But how—" began Shining Pearl.

"I'm going bowling!" Prentiss called back as he ran toward the outcropping.

"Has he lost his mind?" said Ted.

"I think so," said Shining Pearl. She and Ted continued to struggle with the keg. Meanwhile Prentiss ran to the edge of the outcropping and dropped on his belly. He reached out to the top of the closest palm tree where he'd spotted a big bunch of coconuts hanging. He was able to snag one and, pulling with all his strength, yank it loose from the tree. Then he snagged another and another until he'd collected six big coconuts in all.

Cradling them in his arms, he ran back to the slope. The pirates were very close now, but fortunately for Prentiss they were on a steep part of the hill where footing was slippery. The pirate in front was a stocky man with striped pants. Prentiss hefted his biggest coconut in his right hand, drew his arm back and took aim. . . .

Ted and Shining Pearl, still struggling with the keg, heard angry shouts erupt behind them. Ted started to turn.

"Don't look back!" snapped Shining Pearl. "Keep pushing!"

They were getting near the pond now. They passed close by a small pool of bubbling lava. Shining Pearl took note of it, her mind racing ahead, forming a plan. She looked ahead and saw the massive earth dam.

"We're almost there," she said.

"Thank goodness," gasped Ted. "I can't push this much farther."

With one last rush of effort they got the keg up to the mound of dirt and rocks. Behind it lay the new pond, filled by the stream of springwater that normally flowed down Waterfall Hill. The pond had grown quite large; water was spilling out of its sides, running over into the jungle.

The children set the keg on its end. Shining Pearl dropped to her knees and began digging into the dam with her bare hands, throwing rocks and dirt to the side where Ted stood, gasping for air and wiping sweat from his brow.

"No time to rest!" said Shining Pearl. "Quick, find a dry stick, a big one. Stick it into the lava pool back there. When it catches fire, bring it back. And hurry!"

Ted was off running, looking for a stick. Shining Pearl resumed digging. From down the hill she heard shouting, louder now, but she didn't want to turn around to see how close the pirates were.

Prentiss's first try at coconut bowling had worked quite well; the stocky pirate, scrambling to avoid the coconut hurtling down the hill toward him, had slipped and fallen backward, knocking over several pirates behind him. They had slid down, yelping, to the very feet of Hook, almost toppling him over as well.

Prentiss had missed with his second coconut. But with the third he caught a tall, skinny pirate on the shin, causing the pirate to lose his balance and fall. The fourth coconut had missed, but the fifth caught one of the pirates square in the belly, sending him rolling down the hill a good ten yards. So with five coconuts gone, only one pirate—Hook—was still standing. He was still coming up the hill with a look of fury on his face.

Prentiss took careful aim. He drew his arm back, setting his eyes on a spot ten feet in front of the captain and a bit to the right. He flung the coconut hard, putting some spin on it as he let it go. It flew down the hillside, bouncing once . . . twice . . .

It looked as though it would miss Hook. The pirate captain was sure it would miss him; he started to smile, but then, on the third bounce, the spin did its work, and the coconut darted left, right at Hook's ankles. He tried to avoid it but in doing so lost his balance. With a roar of rage, he fell. Prentiss allowed himself a smile. He'd knocked them all down!

But he was also out of coconuts. And the pirates were soon back on their feet and coming up the hill, angrier than ever.

Prentiss glanced up the hill. Ted was stumbling toward the earthen dam, carrying a flaming stick. Shining Pearl was at the base of the dam.

The pirates were getting closer. There was no time to collect more coconuts.

Prentiss took off up the hill with Hook and his men right behind.

Ted trotted up with the burning stick just as Shining Pearl finished digging a hole for the keg in the side of the earth dam. She grabbed a rock and banged it against the cork in the side of the keg to loosen it, then pulled out the cork.

"Help me put it in the hole," she said to Ted. He stuck the burning stick into the dirt, and the two of them wrestled the keg uphill into the hole Shining Pearl had dug. As they moved the keg, powder spilled from the hole, leaving a line of powder in the dirt, running up to the keg.

"Hurry up!" It was Prentiss, running up the hill as fast as he could. The pirates were only a dozen yards behind him. There was no more time.

"Light it!" she said to Ted. He grabbed the stick and touched it to the line of powder just as Prentiss reached them. A coil of black, sparking smoke puffed and swirled and began climbing toward the keg.

"What now?" yelled Ted.

Prentiss and Shining Pearl shouted the answer together:

"RUN!"

CHAPTER 23

NOWHERE to RUN

As THE PIRATES NEARED the earthen dam, Hook saw the children running away from it without the keg. Then he saw the black smoke. He knew right away what it meant.

"THEY LIT THE POWDER!" he bellowed. "RUN!"

The question was, *where* to run. Waterfall Hill was a steep, rocky slope, offering no shelter. On one side—just beyond the huge pond—was a steep drop into the jungle. On the other side was a cliff dropping down to the lagoon. The children were running toward the cliff. For a moment Hook found himself amused by their poor choice. Then, looking around, he realized it was the *only* choice.

"FOLLOW ME!" He started running toward the cliff, followed by his men.

They were too late.

From behind them came a *whoomph*. It was followed, a fraction of second later, by a loud explosion. A huge glob of mud splattered against Hook's back, knocking him down; the other pirates were also flattened. That was a good thing, because the mud was followed by rocks flying through the air fast enough to take off someone's head. Hook and his men, bellydown on the rocky slope, covered their heads as dirt, rocks, and mud rained all around them. After a few seconds it stopped. The pirates, happy to be alive, started to get up.

Then they heard a roaring, rushing sound, the sound of . . .

Water.

They looked up, and there it was. The pond had become a wall of muddy water the height of a man, gushing down the hill straight at them. The pirates started to run from it but managed only a few steps before . . .

WHOOSH!

The huge wave caught the men and swept them off their feet. They tumbled like driftwood scraps, upside down and sideways, arms and legs everywhere. Hook somehow managed to get his head up and, with all his strength, tried to get his feet down, so he could stop himself from being carried by the raging current. His toes touched rock for a moment, then he felt the ground disappear beneath him. Soon, he felt himself falling.

He had gone off the cliff.

Around him, Hook heard his men screaming. He saw the cliff wall only a few feet away, a blur as he shot past it, falling faster and faster. He looked down and caught a glimpse of the dark lagoon, jagged boulders, and other falling bodies. To his horror, he saw that directly below him was a cluster of canoes full of shouting men.

As he hurtled toward it, Hook had barely enough time to close his eyes and shout "LOOK OUT BELOOOOOOOOW!!!"

CHAPTER 24

FALLING WATER

FIGHTING PRAWN, busy battling the mermaids attacking the canoe raft, didn't see the bodies falling. When he heard three loud splashes, his first thought was: *more mermaids.*

Then he saw three heads pop to the surface—two boys, and . . .

Shining Pearl?

Before Fighting Prawn had time to recover from the shock of seeing his daughter in the lagoon, a cascade of water, along with rocks and globs of mud, began to splash into the lagoon all around the raft. Fighting Prawn looked up and saw that there was more—*much* more—coming down from Waterfall Hill. With a shout he dropped his spear, kicked a hissing mermaid out of the way, and dove into the lagoon to save his daughter.

Meanwhile his warriors, seeing that a huge body of water and debris was about to land on them, abandoned their fight with the mermaids and grabbed their paddles, hoping to get away. From overhead they heard the shouts of the falling Hook, who appeared to be heading straight for the raft. Several warriors dropped their paddles and dove overboard.

And then several things happened nearly at once. A gigantic mass of mud and water landed in the lagoon with a thunderous roar, sending up a huge wave that flung the mermaids every which way and lifted the canoe raft like a cork, forcing it rocking and spinning away from the cliff at astonishing speed. This was very fortunate for Hook, who a half-second later plummeted into the lagoon exactly where the raft had been. The raft, carried by the surging wave, was already halfway across the lagoon and still moving fast.

Meanwhile Fighting Prawn, a very strong swimmer, had somehow managed to grab hold of all three

children and pull them under the water. They panicked and struggled to escape, but Fighting Prawn held firm and pulled them deeper, which is what kept them safe from the largest mass of mud and water as it crashed into the lagoon overhead. Finally he brought them to the surface; they gasped for air as the current carried them toward Mermaid Island.

Meanwhile another thing was happening, less obvious to the human eye. The water spilling over Waterfall Hill was *fresh* water, millions of gallons of it. As it poured into the lagoon, it began to flush out the stagnant water that had caused the Blood Tide. Almost immediately, the mermaids in the lagoon began to feel the effects of this change: it was like a drowning person suddenly getting big gulps of fresh air. The mermaids felt much better; the strange anger that had gripped them melted away. They felt *happy* again. They swam, smiling, into the stream of water spilling from Waterfall Hill. They had no interest in fighting the Mollusks or anybody else; they couldn't even remember why they had wanted to.

Unfortunately, not all of the mermaids were in the lagoon. Some of them were on Mermaid Island. They had not felt the fresh water, and the anger still gripped them.

And with every second, as they dragged themselves, hissing with fury, across the rocky ground, they were getting closer to James, Thomas, and Little Scallop.

CHAPTER 25

THE RISING WAVE

WHEN THEY HEARD THE EXPLOSION on Waterfall
Hill, James, Little Scallop, and Thomas were in bad
trouble. They were surrounded, dodging from rock
to rock, staying just ahead of the mermaids. But the
hissing, snarling mermaids kept getting closer and
closer. Soon there would be nowhere for the children to run.

The chase stopped briefly when a loud BOOM
echoed across the lagoon. Everyone, children and
mermaids alike, looked to see what had caused it.
But after a few seconds the mermaids were coming
again. As he avoided them, James kept glancing at

Waterfall Hill. What he saw amazed him. First, three small figures appeared at the edge of the cliff. James recognized them as Ted, Prentiss, and Shining Pearl. They stood there for a moment, and then, to James's shock, they had leaped off the cliff!

A moment later, James saw why: a massive wall of water roared down the mountain. James saw men caught in the rushing water . . . *pirates*, he realized. The surge swept them all, screaming, over the cliff. The mass of water hit the lagoon with the sound of thunder. Once again the mermaids paused to look. What they and James saw was terrifying: heading right toward them was a huge wave. James could see that it was higher than where he stood at the top of Mermaid Island. The entire island would be underwater!

"RUN!!!" he shouted, racing toward Little Scallop and Thomas and grabbing their hands. The three of them sprinted past two mermaids, both staring, hypnotized, at the gigantic oncoming wall of water. James led Thomas and Shining Pearl past them, down the hill in the direction of the wave.

"Why are we going this way?" said Thomas.

"I have an idea," said James. *I hope it works*, he thought.

As they neared the bottom, they saw Teacher. Her back was to them. Two mermaids guarded her, but they, too, were distracted by the sight of the huge wave.

"HELLO!" James shouted.

The mermaids turned to look at him.

"What are you *doing?*" said Little Scallop.

The mermaids were now fully facing the children, turned away from the towering wave rushing toward the island. James tried to figure out how long it would take to reach them. The guard mermaids started to drag themselves toward the children. James, still holding the other children's hands, started running toward the hissing mermaids.

"You're mad!" Little Scallop said, pulling back.

"You've got to trust me!" James said. "Our only hope is to reach Teacher!"

Little Scallop and Thomas, now understanding the plan, ran forward with James. Teacher also understood and began to drag herself toward them. They all came together—children, guard mermaids, and Teacher—at exactly the moment that the wave, with the sound of a hundred roaring locomotives, crashed onto the island.

"TEACHER!" shouted James, but his voice was lost in the thunderous sound. Hanging on to Little Scallop and Thomas, he lunged toward the mermaid, who wrapped her arms around the three children as the water crashed over them. In the next instant the world turned upside down and sideways as the children and Teacher were whirled around inside the churning water, which luckily swept them away from the rocky island into deeper water. Still, James, Thomas, and Shining Pearl thought their lungs would burst as the water held them under for what seemed like forever. But Teacher gripped them tightly and, using her powerful tail, worked her way upward. Finally they reached the surface, where James, Thomas, and Little Scallop took big gulps of air.

James looked back; the wave had passed over Mermaid Island and then receded, leaving its rocks exposed once again. But very near the top of the island, James spied something else: three children he knew well, and standing with them, hugging Shining Pearl, was Fighting Prawn. They were soaking wet but appeared unhurt.

"Father!" shouted Little Scallop, waving her arm. Fighting Prawn and Shining Pearl waved back, as did Ted and Prentiss.

In a few moments, Teacher had towed James, Thomas, and Little Scallop back to Mermaid Island.

Safe! thought James, as they reached the shore. He was about to thank Teacher for saving them, but before he could, she arched her back and dove into the now-fresh waters of the lagoon.

CHAPTER 26

BLUB BLUB BLUB

HOOK, HAVING BEEN SWEPT OFF the cliff, was deep underwater—and he couldn't swim. There had never been any reason for him to; he'd always had a ship beneath him.

But now he was trying desperately to learn. He flailed his arms and legs, only to find himself sinking deeper into the murky depths of the lagoon. He tried to cry for help, but made only a noise that sounded like *BLUB!* as bubbles of precious air escaped from his mouth.

He saw somebody swimming his way. He reached out, thinking it was one of his men, but he recoiled in fear when he realized it was a mermaid. She had heard what Hook's men had not. She swam toward him, her grinning mouth showing rows of razor-sharp teeth. Hook panicked, trying frantically to swim away. But he only made himself sink faster.

"*BLUB!!*" he shouted, letting more air escape his lungs.

The mermaid swam straight at him. Hook reached for his sword, but in the water his arms moved too slowly. So he raised his fists prepared to box her.

But the mermaid was a magnificent swimmer, almost as fluid as the water itself. At the last second she darted around Hook. He spun to face her, but she wasn't there—only streaks of tiny bubbles forming circles around him, like the rings of Saturn.

Suddenly Hook felt hands slip under his arms from behind. Hook was too weak to struggle now; he was blacking out from lack of air.

She's going to squeeze all the air out of me! he thought.

But instead she gently wrapped her arms around him. Suddenly Hook felt himself rapidly being lifted up—*up!*—toward the surface. The water grew brighter; the surface was a glowing mirror. Hook felt the thrusts of her powerful tail pushing them higher and higher.

His face broke through, and he gulped for air. Now the mermaid was towing him toward shore.

She's rescuing me!

Hook looked around. It was the same all over the lagoon: smiling mermaids pulling Mollusk warriors and pirates to shore or to the Mollusks' overturned raft.

In a minute Hook felt sand beneath his feet. He scrambled, getting his legs under him. Land had never felt so good.

His rescuer lingered a few feet from shore, apparently waiting to make sure he made it to the beach safely.

Hook turned to her, and as their eyes met, he spoke two words that he had never—not once—uttered or even thought of uttering. Two words that to him sounded almost like a foreign language. But they were the two most honest words he'd ever spoken.

"Thank you," he said.

The mermaid's smile grew wider.

And she swam away.

CHAPTER 27

THE BEST DAY

By THE NEXT DAY, the lagoon no longer held any tinge of red; it was back to its usual shimmering, sparkling blue. The waterfall tumbled into the lagoon from Waterfall Hill, making a pleasant splashing sound. Teacher and the other mermaids were sunning on the rocks off Mermaid Island, having taken a long swim.

Gathered on the beach were Little Scallop and the boys, who had been led there by Fighting Prawn. For a few moments everybody simply enjoyed the scene, although James shivered a little when he thought about fleeing from hissing needle-toothed mermaids on the now-peaceful little island.

Finally, Fighting Prawn turned to the children and broke the silence.

"You have done well," he said. "You brought peace to the island. You saved the mermaids. We would have hurt them, killed them perhaps, if you hadn't brought back the waterfall, which drove the Blood Tide away."

"Do the mermaids remember attacking us?" asked Shining Pearl.

"I doubt that they remember much, if anything, of their meanness," said Fighting Prawn. "When the fresh water returned, they quickly became themselves again and saved many of us, pirates and Mollusks alike. But you children were the ones who saved them. So it is you that the tribe wishes to thank."

Fighting Prawn raised his hand. As he did, the entire Mollusk clan emerged from the jungle surrounding the lagoon. One of the women walked up to Fighting Prawn and handed him six necklaces, from each of which hung a perfect pink sand dollar.

James blushed. "We didn't exactly know what we were doing," he said.

"Perhaps not," said Fighting Prawn. "But what you did was right, and it took great courage. You saved the mermaids, and you surely saved some of us. You saved our village from those foolish pirates. You saved the lagoon. In truth, you saved our island." He turned to Shining Pearl and Little Scallop. "And my daughters have brought honor to our family." He knelt and hugged the two girls, who both beamed with pride. Then Fighting Prawn stood and said, "I'm very proud of all of you. By your actions yesterday, you have earned yourselves the title of warrior."

Shining Pearl's face lit with excitement. "Warrior? Really?"

Fighting Prawn said, "You and your friends will be honorary warriors."

"Oh . . . *honorary*," said Shining Pearl.

Ted said excitedly, "I've never been a warrior before."

Thomas said, "Does that mean we get to wear face paint?"

Fighting Prawn chuckled. "We'll see," he said. Then he beckoned to the other Mollusks, who gathered in a semicircle around the children. They watched with big smiles as Fighting Prawn put the necklaces, one by one, over the children's heads. Then, in a booming voice, the chief said: "For conquering the Blood Tide and maintaining peace on our island, I declare that these brave children are honorary warriors of the Mollusk tribe!"

The Mollusks erupted in a cheer that echoed across the lagoon. Raising their arms, they chanted a special chant in celebration of the new warriors. From the island, the mermaids were waving.

James looked around, taking it all in—the hot sun, the waving mermaids, the sparkling waterfall pouring from Waterfall Hill into the pristine lagoon, the necklace around his neck, his friends by his side—everyone smiling. James smiled, and he looked at Shining Pearl, who was smiling too. They were both thinking the same thing:

This is the best day of my life.